RAPTOR
FURY VIPERS MC: DUBLIN CHAPTER

BROOKE SUMMERS

First Edition published in 2024

Text Copyright © Brooke Summers

Edits by Farrant Editing

Proofreading by Author bunnies

All rights reserved.

The moral right of the author has been asserted. No part of this publication may be reproduced, stored in or introduced into a retrieval system, or transmitted, in any form or by any means (electronic, mechanical, photocopying, recording or otherwise), nor be otherwise circulated in any form of binding or cover other than that in which it is published without the prior written permission of the author. Any person who does any unauthorized act in relation to this publication may be liable to criminal prosecution and civil claims for damages.

All characters in this publication are fictitious and any resemblance to real persons, living or dead, is purely coincidental.

CONTENT
PLEASE READ CAREFULLY.

There are elements and themes within this book that some readers might find extremely upsetting.

Please check out my website for that list of potentially harmful topics. Please heed these as this book contains some heavy topics that some readers could find damaging.

www.brookesummersbooks.com

CHAPTER 1
RAPTOR

Eighteen Months Ago

"You haven't called," the bartender says, hurt lacing her words.

"No need," Pyro bites out. He's not interested and has made that more than clear, but she's not listening. "Don't you have work to do?" he snarls and I hide my amusement.

He had a night with her a while back and the woman has not got the damn message. She's still holding out for another night, but Pyro's a man who's one and done. He won't go back for seconds. Even if he were to ever do so, it wouldn't be with someone so clingy. We find women who know the score. Py and I aren't interested in finding an old lady. Not yet anyway. There are enough of our brothers who have been bitten by the love bug, and I'll be fucking damned if I become one of them. I've watched how that shit plays out, and not one of their journeys was smooth sailing. Fuck no. Just find me a woman for the night and I'll be happy.

The bartender grins at Pyro's brush off. No matter how harshly he spurns her advances, she remains interested.

"Brother," I say, trying to conceal my laughter. "You were an asshole, man, but shit, she's not goin' to give a fuck. She'll be back. Best way to show her you're not interested is to find someone else to fuck tonight. She'll soon get the hint."

I throw my head back and laugh when he starts to scan the crowd in the bar. My man is on the hunt for a woman and it's about damn time. It's been months since he's been on the prowl. While most of the brothers will fuck frequently, especially the club whores, Pyro's not into it and he'll go months without finding a woman to fuck.

"Damn," I say with a grin. "Pyro's on the prowl. Fuckin' hell, man, tonight's shapin' up to be fuckin' fantastic."

Pyro and I met when he first joined the Fury Vipers. He's the nearest thing I have to a brother; my closest friend. We have shared women in the past, multiple times. It's a fun time all around. Neither Py nor I are territorial about the women, and we both know that when the time comes for us to have an old lady, there'll be no sharing.

A small woman bumps into Pyro, and when I turn to see her, my entire body jolts at the other woman standing beside her. Her long black hair falls in soft waves down her back, complimenting her black dress, which is so short, I'm pretty sure if she were to bend over, I'd see her pussy. My cock thickens at the thought. She's gorgeous; without a doubt one of the most beautiful women I have ever met. She's got pouty lips that are painted the brightest of reds, and her eyes are dark and smoldering. Christ, who is this woman?

"Jesus, Chloe, are you okay?" she says to her friend.

I'm in fucking love. That velvety, thick Irish accent is a zap to my cock. Christ... Never before have I been so enamored with a woman.

"I'm so sorry," her friend, Chloe, says. Her accent is thick, but it isn't as velvety as her friend's.

"You drunk, darlin'?" I ask with a raised brow.

Pyro spares me a glance, and there's a whole lot of possessiveness in that glance. I know the feeling. I wouldn't want him near the black-haired beauty. I can't help but chuckle. What the fuck is going on with us?

"No," Chloe says with disgust. "Your alcohol isn't that strong. Do you water it down or something?"

Pyro laughs. It's fucking good to see my brother happy. It's been a while since I've seen him so carefree.

"Let me guess," Pyro says, still laughing. "What they say is true: you Irish know how to handle your liquor."

Chloe rolls her eyes. "Like it's hard?"

The gorgeous, raven-haired woman nods. "So, what's fun to do around here? We only have a few days left before we leave. You two look like you'd be a great time." She smiles brightly. "I'm Mallory, and this is my girl, Chloe."

Oh, now it's about to get more interesting. I have her name. I flash her a smile, pleased as fuck at the interest in her eyes. "I'm Raptor, darlin'. It's a fuckin' pleasure to meet you."

Mallory's smile widens. "Oh no, I'm guessing the pleasure is going to be mine later."

My cock is thicker than it's been in a long-ass time. This woman is about to have the best fucking night of her life. "Fuckin' guarantee it, darlin'."

I take Mallory's hand and lead her through the throngs of people at the bar, toward the VIP section. This bar is owned by the Italian mafia, and whenever we come here, we're always able to get a seat in the VIP section. Over the years, the Italian and Irish mafia have grown close to the Vipers. They helped us out when we were in a spot of trouble.

"What brings you to New York?" I ask once we're seated. Mallory slides in beside me, and Chloe sits beside Pyro. It seems as though we've both found our one for the night.

"Family," Chloe replies. "I'm going to Chicago after this to see my family, but Mallory and I have just finished school, and we decided to come to New York for a holiday before I need to meet the family."

Mallory nods. "Yep. It's been fun to let loose in the big city. Dublin's great and all, but the shopping here is amazing. I've had to add on extra luggage for my flight home."

I'm trying to focus on Mallory, but Chloe's words hits me. "Y'all just said you're finished with school... You meant college, right?" I ask, hoping like hell that I've missed something.

Chloe shakes her head. "No."

My entire body stills as Pyro's gaze meets mine.

"How old are you?" he questions.

"Eighteen," she tells us, and while I'm relieved they're of legal age, I'm a fucking lot older than that. I'm thirty-four and Mallory's eighteen. There's a sixteen year age gap between us.

"You've got to be twenty-one to be in the club and drink," Pyro says pointedly.

She raises a brow. "Oh? And are you going to tell on me?"

I chuckle. Christ, these Irish women are a hoot.

"So, you're in a motorcycle club?" Mallory asks, twisting her body so that she's facing me. "That's cool."

I grin. She's fucking sweet and so damn sexy. "It is. There's nothin' better than bein' on your bike with an open road in front of you."

She nods. "I get it. My passion was dancing, but I lost the love for it. I need to find something that gives me that feeling, you know?"

"Yep. Trust me, darlin', once you find it, you'll know. What are your plans now that you've finished school?"

She sighs. "College, I suppose. I'm just not all that academic. I'd rather not waste my life away by sitting in a classroom."

I chuckle. Christ, this woman is exactly like me. We have a lot in common in that sense. I wasn't acadmeic, I couldn't imaging being stuck in college, that's just not how I could ever invisige my life.

"You wanna get out of here?" Pyro asks, and there's no chill in that man's voice at all. He's laying everything on the table.

Chloe bites her bottom lip and glances over at Mallory. Not a fucking word is said between the two, but there's some sort of communication going on, that's for sure.

"Yes," she tells Pyro, and he doesn't hang around. He pulls her from her seat and within seconds they're leaving the club.

Mallory's laughter is soft and velvety. "I'm glad she's having fun."

"What about you, darlin'? You want to have fun?"

Her eyes are bright and her smile wide. "Definitely," she breathes.

"Come, Mallory," I say and reach for her hand. The moment she places her palm against mine, I jolt. Christ, she's fucking gorgeous.

I'M edgy as fuck as we make our way up to Mallory's hotel room. Sitting in the back of the cab with her pressed against me was enough to snap almost every ounce of restraint I possess. This woman has no fucking idea how much I want her; no fucking clue what she's getting herself in to.

"Raptor," she says thickly, her hands shaking she tries to unlock the hotel room door.

I press against her back, and the little whimper that escapes her has my cock twitching. I slide the keycard from her hands and unlock the door myself.

I need to be inside of her. My cock is aching.

The second we're inside the room, I kick the door shut behind us, and then she's on me. I fucking love that she's not afraid to go for what she wants. Our lips collide, frantic and consuming, as my hands skim along her body. Fuck, she's got curves in all the right places. She's pulling at my shirt, leaving scratches on my skin that only fuel the fire raging within me.

I grip her hair harshly, turning her head to the side, and free my lips from hers. "What the fuck are you doing to me?"

She's fucking bewitched me—that's all I can think. I'm not usually like this. I don't ever run this hot. But with Mallory, I'm close to the fucking edge.

She smiles up at me, her eyes glinting with lustful fire. "I want you, Raptor."

Fuck, I feel the fucking same. All I want is her, and I can't deny that any longer.

With a growl, I release her hair and rip my shirt off, tossing it aside. My hands slide around her waist as I lift her off the ground. She wraps her legs around me, the heat between her thighs seeping through my pants and warming my skin, causing my cock to throb with need.

Panting heavily, she gasps, "I want you, Raptor. Please."

I carry her toward the bed, my determination unwavering. I need to be inside her, to feel her around me, to claim her completely. I throw her down on the bed, her back hits the sheets, my eyes locked with hers. I can see the hunger and desire reflected in her eyes, mirroring my own.

I strip her from her dress and panties, leaving her lying before me naked. I reach down and remove my belt with a swift move, letting it fall to the floor. Then, I unbuckle my belt and push my pants down, my hard cock springing free, pulsing with need. Mallory's eyes widen at the sight, before she reaches out to touch me, her fingers brushing against my length.

"Oh," she whispers, her voice breaking with desire. "Can I touch you?" she asks hesitantly.

My cock twitches at her words. Instead of answering, I grab her hand and guide it to my aching cock, watching as her eyes widen again then close in pleasure.

"You like that, don't you?" I breathe, my voice low and rough.

"Yes," she moans, her grip tightening around my length. "I want to feel you inside me."

Fuck, I need this. I need to feel her tight heat around me, her soft skin beneath my hands. I slide my pants off the rest of the way and kick them away, then I crawl up her body, my cock hovering over her, my hands gripping her waist.

"Fuck," I snarl as I thrust deep into her tight, wet channel.

A piercing scream rents the air, and I still; bottomed out inside of her. I glance down at her, seeing the tears in her eyes, and it hits me. Fuck, she's a virgin.

"Why didn't you tell me?" I ask. What the hell?

Mallory looks up at me, her eyes wide with fear and embarrassment.

"I'm sorry," she whispers, her voice trembling. "I thought... I thought it would be okay."

She swallows hard. I'm bracing myself on my hands and arms as I hold myself still, waiting for her to get accustomed to my cock.

"Please," she begs. "Please, Raptor."

I grit my teeth. "Are you sure?"

She nods. "Please," she pleads.

I pull out slowly and thrust deep into her. Christ, she feels so good.

"Oh fuck," I groan, sliding my cock in and out of her tight heat. I can feel her trembling beneath me, her nails digging into my back as she holds on for dear life.

"That's it," I growl, grabbing her hips and setting a rhythm that has us both gasping and moaning. My cock slides in and out of her, filling her completely as she takes me deeper and deeper.

"I'm so close," she whispers, her voice shaking. "Please, just keep going. I need this."

I can't hold back anymore. I thrust harder and deeper, feeling her body start to shake and tremble beneath me. Her walls tighten around me, and that's all it takes to send me over the edge.

"Fuck!" I roar, my release crashing over me like a tidal wave. I thrust into her one last time, my cock twitching as I come harder than ever before.

Mallory gasps, her body convulsing beneath me as we both reach our climax together. I collapse on top of her, my breathing ragged. I press a kiss to the side of her neck, my heart pounding in my chest.

"Once I've recovered," I tell her, "we'll be doing that again."

Her laughter causes my skin to tingle with goosebumps.

"Okay, Raptor," she replies. "Whatever you say."

"Trust me, Mallory, I'm going to want to do that over and over again. How long until you leave to go back home?"

"A few days," she murmurs.

"Then you're mine until then."

The grin that I get in return is blinding. I don't need to ask her if that's what she wants because her face gives her feelings away without her needing to say a fucking word.

Damn it, there's a heaviness on my chest at the thought of her leaving. Crap. What the fuck is going on with me?

CHAPTER 2
MALLORY

Fifteen Months Ago

My hands shake as I stare at the test. I'm in disbelief. What the hell am I going to do?

"Mallory," my best friend whispers, "it's going to be okay," she assures me.

"How?" I cry. "God, Jess, I'm eighteen, pregnant, and the father lives on the other side of the world. What the hell am I going to do?"

She gives me that smile, the one that reaches her eyes. It's so bright, so filled with love that I know that whatever happens, I'm going to be okay. It's the smile Jess used on me throughout our childhood, when things got tough. She always accompanied it with a promise that everything would be okay. "Trust me, no matter what, you've got this. Whatever you decide, you're not alone. You've never been alone. You have me and Chloe. We'll support you through it all."

I sigh. "That's just it, Jess, both you and Chloe have been through hell and back. You're still living in your hell. I can't add any more stress onto either of you."

She shakes her head, the blonde strands of her hair falling down her back. "Trust me, nothing you ever do would bring me stress. You have been my light throughout my darkness. I would do anything for you, Mal. You know that."

"I love you, Jess," I whisper. She's been my best friend since junior infants. We've been inseparable since the day we met. Our mas became friends because of us. So when Jess' ma died, it was hard for all of us. but we stuck together and overcame the worst of our grief. I would do anything for Jess and vice-versa. Helping with a baby however, is a big thing to ask someone, and I'm not sure if I could ever do that to her or Chloe.

"I love you too. Now, how far along are you? Do you know?" she asks.

I shake my head. "I don't," I whisper. "Either around a few weeks or three months."

She raises her brow. "That's a huge difference, Mal," she says, but there's no anger or reprimand in her voice, just concern.

I nod. "It is. With everything that's been going on recently, I lost track of a lot of things."

I feel guilty, so damn guilty all the time, especially ever since Chloe was kidnapped. It was just days after we had said our goodbyes at the airport in New York. I was returning home and Chloe was moving on to Chicago to meet with more family. She had asked if I wanted to go with her. I should have said yes. Had I done, maybe she wouldn't have been kidnapped and hurt.

Not only do I have guilt over Chloe, but I feel so much guilt over everything Jess has been through and is still going through. The moment her ma was buried, her father turned abusive toward her. I should have told someone, but I was fourteen and stupid. Now, at the age of eighteen, I know I fucked up, and I can't help but think that I could have stopped everything she's been through had spoken up all those years ago. But I made Jess a promise. I swore that I wouldn't tell anyone about the abuse she suffers at the hands of her father. I know that if I ever did, she'd never speak to me again, and I can't take that risk. I'm the only person she has who will care for her if things get bad again. I regret making that promise and keeping it to this day. I wish I could tell someone, let someone know that Jess is still going through hell. But I won't ever betray my best friend. I could never do that, espeically as I'm the only person she trusts implicitly.

Jess smiles at me. "We've all been a little preoccupied lately so no one can fault you for that." She takes a deep breath and reaches for my hand. "Why don't we get you an appointment with the doctor and get the dates, and then we can go from there."

I nod, glad to have her at my side. I couldn't imagine going through this alone.

"Are you going to tell Chloe?" she asks softly.

I sigh. "I'm not sure." I sigh, before telling her my frustrations with the situation. "I don't have

Raptor's number. Besides, what am I going to do? He lives in New York, for Christ's sake. I live here. I'm not moving." I shake my head, my stomach churning. The thought of leaving makes me want to throw up. I can't leave Jess. I just can't. "His entire life is in New York, Jess. What do I say? Call him up and be like, 'Hey Raptor, I don't know if you remember me but I'm the Irish girl you spent a few nights with when I visited New York, and then again when you were in Dublin. I just wanted to let you know I'm pregnant'."

I bug my eyes out at her. It sounds stupid and ridiculous. What on earth am I going to do?

Jess wraps her arms around me and pulls me into a tight hug. "Don't panic," she whispers. "Everything will work out as it should."

For someone who's been tortured for so long, she has one of the most positive outlooks on life when it's just the two of us. I know she wants to escape, but she's scared of what her father will do if she does, and I can't lie, I am too. That man is a monster. He's vile and awful. I wish he'd die and set Jess free. It's not a nice thought, but Thomas Grace is a mean old bastard who needs to be put down.

"I can't tell Chloe," I confess. "She's with Pyro now, and no matter what, they'll tell Raptor, whether I'm ready for that or not. Until I find the courage to tell him myself, I can't be open with her."

Jess nods. "I get it. It's why Chloe doesn't know about my dad. If she did, she'd tell her mam and dad, and the last thing I need is my cousin losing her mind and telling her brother. I love Maverick. He's been sweet to me the last year or so. But I know if he found out what Dad was doing, he'd kill him." She sighs. "I can't have that on my conscience."

Jess has such a sweet and caring nature that even the thought of someone hurting her dad—the man who has abused her for the past four years, who's set her on fire, who's made her watch as he rapes and murders people—makes her want to cry. She wants to see the best in people and I admire that, but sometimes people don't deserve to have forgiveness, nor do they deserve grace, and her dad is a man who deserves neither. The sooner that fucker dies the better. I'll be dancing and celebrating the day he does, and I have no doubt there'll be a lot more people doing the same.

"Someday, Jess, you're going to realize your dad isn't the man you want him to be, and it's going to hurt, but you'll be better for it."

She gives me a small smile. "Maybe," she says, though I know she doesn't believe it. She'll always look for the good in people. "What are you going to say to your mam?"

I inwardly groan. I love my ma, I really do, but she's spent her life putting her work ahead of me. When I was younger, I used to spend the majority of my time at Jess' house because Ma would be working and I wasn't old enough to look after myself. As I got older, I was able to stay home. I could do whatever I wanted. Ma didn't care because she was never around. I doubt she'll even care that I'm pregnant.

"I will tell her, but I want to find out how far along I am and then go from there."

Jess nods. "Let me know if you need me to come to the appointment, and when you speak to your mam."

My heart fills with so much love. God, what did I ever do to deserve a friend like her? She's always at my side no matter what.

"Thank you," I whisper, relieved and grateful

that I have one person who will be with me through it all.

"Ma?" I call out as I enter the house.

She's finally home after being gone for two weeks. Seeing her car parked out front has set dread in my stomach. Today is the day I have to tell her that she's going to be a grandmother. Sometimes I'll see her once every few months, other times she'll be home every weekend. It really depends on her job. She works for a tech company here in Dublin, but they have clients all over the world. Ma deals with them, which is why she's always traveling. It's been hard not having her here, but I get that she's doing everything she can to provide for us.

"In here, love," she calls back. "I have some dinner for us. I hope you're hungry; I've gone a little overboard."

I laugh. She always does, but that means there's plenty of leftovers. I walk into the kitchen and see that she's not wrong. There are bags of takeout food for us. Way too many. "Who're you feeding Ma, the five thousand?"

She reaches for a dish cloth and throws it at me. "Hush you," she says with a smile as she rounds the kitchen island and pulls me into a hug. "Missed you, love. How have you been?"

I nod. "I'm good," I say and then pull in a ragged breath. "Ma, do you think we could talk for a minute?"

Her brows knit together and she takes my hand. "Of course. Is everything okay?"

I lift my shoulders and shrug. "I don't know. I'm pregnant."

Her lips part into an 'O' shape and she stares at me. There's no anger or disappointment in her eyes, just shock. "And how are you feeling? Any morning sickness?"

I shake my head. "No, none. It's been okay. I didn't even know until last week. I had a scan on Monday. I'm twelve weeks."

It happened when I was in New York. I should have kept track of my period. I should have known something was off about my body. But I didn't. Instead, I found out at twelve weeks, after I realized it had been months since I last purchased tampons.

Ma's face breaks out into a smile. "Oh, love, that's wonderful news. Are you dealing with it okay?" she questions as she leads me to the stools at the kitchen island. "I know it must have been a huge shock. You could have called me, Mallory. I'm always a call away if you need to talk."

I stare at her, wondering where the hell the woman went that would tell me to only call if there's an emergency. Hell, why is she happy about this? I thought for sure she'd flip out.

"Honey, I'm your ma. I'm always here if you need me."

I can't help the emotion that wells up. Tears spring to my eyes, and I can't hold back. Ugly sobs spill from me. Everything I've bottled up over the past few years pours out of me as I cry. Ma's arms wrap around me and she holds me tight, promising me that everything is going to be okay.

"I thought you abandoned me," I cry between sobs. "That you didn't want to speak to me unless you were home."

I feel her kiss my head as she rocks me in her arms. "Oh, my girl," she whispers. "No, no. God no. You are the most important person in my life. I have worked my ass off to give us the best life possible.

Being a single mam isn't easy, love, and I hate that you feel that I abandoned you. It wasn't my intention. I love you, Mallory. God, I love you with every piece of my soul. Never doubt that. I'm so sorry."

Together, we both sob. My life has been lonely. I've always felt alone, other than when I was with my friends. I thought she didn't want me, that she didn't care about me. I was wrong. Boy, was I wrong. I just wish she had told me this years ago. Maybe our relationship would have been better.

"I promise you, love, I'll do better. I'll do so much better," she swears as she holds me tight.

I sink into her embrace. Unsure if I can trust her words, but I'm going to, she's all that I have and I need her right now.

"Come on, Mal," she says softly. "Let's go eat and we can talk."

I help her dish out the dinner and then we move to the sitting room, where I take a seat on the sofa. Ma sits opposite me, her eyes red and puffy from crying.

"I'm so sorry," she begins. "Honestly, Mal, had I known what you were thinking and feeling, I wouldn't have gone away so often. You've always been an independent girl, wanting to take on the world."

I scoff. "I had to, Ma. You were gone from the age of five onwards. I had no choice but to take on the world alone."

She nods. "I guess I was naive in thinking everything would work out, that the money I was making was more than enough for us to be happy."

"Ma, I appreciate you working your ass off to provide for us. I'm grateful that you do whatever it takes to support me financially. But in the process of doing that, you forgot about me."

"I did and I'm so fucking sorry, love. So damn sorry. I know there's nothing that can make up for all the years I have missed with you, but I'm hoping you'll allow me to show you I'm here for you no matter what."

I want to believe her, but I'm not sure if I'm willing to get my hopes up only for her to dash them without a care. Still, I nod. She's my ma, my family, and I know that when the time comes for me to have this baby, I'm going to need as many people around me as possible.

"I will," I assure her. "I just hope you're not angry."

Her mouth opens in shock, you say something like: Her mouth opens and her eyebrows jump halfway up her forehead. "God no, I'm not angry. I'm disappointed with myself, and I'm so very proud of you for opening up to me. I'm sorry it's taken years for us to have this conversation. It should have been had when you were younger. I'm sorry."

"It's okay," I say, not wanting to talk about this anymore. She's apologized and she's trying to fix it. That's all I can ask for, all anyone can ask for.

"Now, Mal, what about the father—"

I shake my head, cutting her off. "He lives in New York."

Her smile fades, but her expression is filled with understanding. "Whenever you're ready to tell him, I'll be right there with you."

"How do you tell a man they're going to be a dad?" I ask, hoping she can part with some wisdom so I can get through this.

She gives me a soft smile. "I don't know, Mallory, but I know when you're ready, you'll tell him."

I sigh. I really hope she's right. "I don't even have his number, Ma."

She grins. "That's okay. You say the word and we'll find it. We won't stop until we have it."

I sigh in relief. Finding out I was pregnant was the biggest shock of my life. I thought I'd have to do this alone, but I have Ma, and I have Jess. Once I muster up the courage, I'll call Raptor. Until then, I need to consider what I'm going to do to raise this baby. I don't even have a job right now. Hell, I've never had a job. I need to start planning for the future.

I feel more settled now that Ma knows. It's going to be hard, but I have a feeling everything will be okay. I hope.

CHAPTER 3
RAPTOR

"You good, brother?" Stag questions. "You've been mopin' around for a while now; ever since you got back from Ireland, now that I think about it. It's been a few weeks. What's goin' on?"

I shake my head. "Nothin'," I lie.

I know exactly what the fuck is wrong with me. Mallory. I thought spending time apart from her would make me feel less uneasy, but it hasn't worked. The woman is constantly on my mind. It's something I never expected, but fuck, she's a witch and I'm spellbound. That's the only way to describe how I'm feeling. Never, not fucking ever, have I felt this way about anyone before. Now, I'm contemplating what to do. I want her, I really do. I've thought long and fucking hard about what it would mean and what I'd have to sacrifice to be with her, and it's fucked up beyond anything I've ever known. How do you give up everything you've worked your ass off for? How do you give up your family, your brotherhood, for a woman? You don't, and yet that's what I'm contemplating doing.

"Yeah, whatever you say, brother," Stag laughs. "But we all know you better than that. We all know what that look on your face means. You've found your woman. So what's the problem?"

I glare at the fucker. He's awful fucking chatty today. "Where's Kins?" I ask, wanting to know where his old lady is.

He scowls at me. "Busy. Now, what's happened?" he asks. "You were fine, then you went to Ireland, and ever since you came back you've been like a fucking bull. So what gives?"

"My woman lives in Ireland," I tell him through gritted teeth. "So tell me, man, what's goin' to happen?"

He runs his hand down his beard. "That's shit, brother. You serious about her?"

"Thinkin' about going nomad and movin' to

Ireland," I say, letting him know just how fucking serious I am.

His eyes widen. "Alright, brother, I get it. Trust me, if it were Kins, I'd be finding out ways to be with her. What's your woman's name?"

"Mallory," I tell him. She's my raven-haired beauty and I fucked up. I truly fucked up.

"Have you spoken to her since you've been home?" he asks.

I shake my head. "Don't have her cell number. I don't even know her last name. The only things I do know is that she's eighteen, she's Chloe's best friend, and she's fucking bewitched me."

The fucker throws his head back and laughs. "You really are gone, aren't you?"

I flip him off. "Don't even know where to start looking, brother."

Stag grins. "Relax. It'll all work out," he assures me.

I raise a brow. "Yeah? And how do you see that happening?"

"Py's goin' to need a VP, brother. He's goin' to need to have some brothers at his back. Who's to say one can't be you?"

"Move to Ireland?" I ask. It's something I thought about, but I never considered it definite.

"Pyro needs a VP, brother. You movin' is goin' to strengthen the club over there. It'll mean you won't lose your club or your brothers, and you'll get your woman."

I sigh. "You think everyone will vote?" I ask, wondering if I need to put the word out. I know that if I let them know this is what I want, my brothers will be behind me one hundred percent, even if it means losing me.

He lifts his shoulders. "Some have taken it hard that Py's gone to Ireland as it is, but I have no doubt that if it's truly what you want, then it'll happen."

"True," I say as I give him a chin lift and move away. Fuck, this is a lot to think about.

Two weeks later

"YOU GOOD, BROTHER?" I ask Wrath as I slap him on the back. "You're lookin' awful chipper this mornin'." He's been spending a lot of time at Hayley's house and I know that this is what he's wanted. It's taken a fucking long time for him to get to this point.

He glares at me, his eyes narrowed. "Yeah?"

My grin widens. There's nothing better than getting a rise out of my brothers, and Wrath's awful touchy about Hayley and Eva. It's about damn time they got their shit together. Although, Pyro's gonna lose his mind when he finds out.

"The fuckin' women are ecstatic. You're finally claimin' Hayley. That's all they've wanted for years, and now they have it. Not to mention, Eva's tellin' everyone you're her daddy."

Wrath raises a brow at me. He's not a man who backs down. "You got a problem with that?" he clips out.

"No problem, brother." I grin. "I'm pleased for you, and I know Py will be too." That, of course, is after he punches him. I laugh at his raised brow. "He will be—once he gets over the fact you're fuckin' his sister."

He starts to walk away. "Church," he says with a shake of his head.

I follow behind him, noting that Ace, our prez, is already waiting for us.

Once we're all settled, Ace starts off the meeting, giving a rundown on everything that's on the horizon. Everyone's buzzing with excitement.

Once Ace has finished, I take a deep breath. "I have somethin' I want to say," I start and watch as Ace waves for me to continue. "I've been thinkin' about this a lot. With Pyro now startin' the newest chapter in Ireland, he's going to need some brothers with him. I want to be one of them."

Silence spreads around the room. All eyes are wide and shocked, and all of them on me.

Mayhem chuckles. "You want to see that woman again."

Anger whips through me. "Leave Mallory out of this," I growl, glaring at the ass before turning back to Ace and waiting for his reaction.

"You sure this is what you want?" Prez asks, and I nod. I've been thinking about this for weeks. Fucking weeks. It's what I want. I have no family other than this club and going to Ireland doesn't mean I'll be losing it. "Then we put it to a vote," he says. "Those in favor, say aye."

Wrath is the first to voice his agreement. We've spoken about this on multiple occasions. Wrath is someone I trust wholeheartedly. He's my brother, but he's closer than most. The only other person I'm closer to is Pyro. Gratitude fills me as every single brother agrees with this move. Now I need to get my ass in gear for the move, and then find Mallory.

Once it's been voted on, Wrath begins to talk, letting everyone know that he's claiming Hayley. It's been a fucking long time coming, about five years or so now. But it's damn time they got their shit together.

I know it's going to take some time before I can move. There's shit to be done. But my chest feels fucking lighter. It's only a matter of time before I get to Ireland and to Mallory.

"Hey, brother," Stag says once we leave church, "you got a sec?"

I stop and wait for him. "Everythin' okay?" I question.

He nods. "Everythin' is good. I had Kins talk with Chloe," he says as he reaches into his pocket and pulls out a piece of paper. "Mallory's number," he informs me.

I raise a brow. "You tryin' to matchmake, bro?"

His laughter is deep. "No, but I'm not goin' to watch you lose your woman 'cause you're too chicken shit to call up Chloe and get Mallory's number. So I did it for you—well, Kins did."

I take the number from him. "'Preciate it, brother," I say thickly, gratitude filling every single word I say.

"Talk to your woman, Rap, let her know that you'll be comin' to see her. Tell her she's got time to run if she needs it." The fucker throws his head back and starts laughing.

I flip him off, but I know he's just joking around. My brothers know I want Mallory. They've known it since the moment I met her. There's just something different about her. She's got me hook, line and sinker. There was never any going back. Not for me.

I move toward my room, my fingers curled around the piece of paper that holds Mallory's number. Fuck, I'm glad Stag had Kins do this, though I would have got around to doing it eventually. I just needed to sort my shit out.

The second I'm in my room, I reach for my cell and hit the numbers on the dial pad, remembering from when I was in Ireland to add the 00353 prefix to call an Irish number. The second I hit call, my stomach clenches.

"Hello?" I hear her soft Irish lilt over the phone. "Hello?"

"Mallory," I say thickly.

There's a sharp intake of breath followed by, "Raptor?"

"Yeah, darlin', it's me. I got your number from Chloe. You good?"

"I'm good," she breathes. "I didn't expect to hear from you. How are you?"

Fuck, that softness in her voice has my cock thickening. "Even better now that I've heard your voice."

Her laughter is soft and melodic. "Still the charmer, I see. How's New York?"

"Same as it always is. How's Dublin?"

"Rainy," she replies, still smiling. "I love that you called, Raptor, but I'm not sure why."

I get why she's uncertain about it all. We had sex—fantastic sex—but we live across the world from one another.

"I wanted to speak to you. It's fucked up, ain't it—how deep you've dug yourself into me?"

Silence spreads through the line. "Raptor,"

she says softly. "You have no idea how hard it was to walk away from you again. I thought you wanted a clean break. That's what you said, right?"

I run a hand over my face and sigh. "Yeah, that's what I said," I say through clenched teeth. "But it's a lot fucking harder said than done."

"Yeah," she replies. "It's been hard. You're not the only one who feels this way."

I grin. Hearing those words lets me know I'm on the right track. "What if I told you I'd be seeing you soon?"

"Soon? How soon?" she asks, a hint of excitement in her voice.

"I've got shit to work out here so it could take me a couple of months, maybe a little longer, but I'll be over to see you soon." I wish it were sooner, but my brothers and I have to sort out logistics and shit before that can happen.

"That'll be cool. You've got to let me know when you're in town," she says, her tone a little distant. "I've got to go. Ma's calling me. It was really good to hear from you, Raptor. Don't be a stranger, yeah?"

The call ends and I'm left staring at my cell wondering what the fuck is going on. I get the sense that something isn't right. There's no fucking way I've got this situation wrong. Mallory isn't a woman who would play around. Yet there's something off about how she was acting.

Fuck, what the hell is wrong with me? That woman has got me in knots.

Soon, I'll be in Ireland, where I will find out what the hell is going on.

CHAPTER 4
MALLORY

"Are you okay?" Ma asks as we sit on the plastic chairs in the waiting room.

Today's the day of my scan. I'm beyond nervous, but I'm excited too. It's sometimes still hard to wrap my head around the fact I'm pregnant. I'm thankful Ma's here with me, trying to make up for not being around when I was younger. "I'm sound," I reply with a smile. "Excited to see the baby."

She reaches for my hand, giving it a reassuring squeeze. "I am too. I'm excited to be a granny," she breathes, her eyes bright with happiness. "Thank you for letting me be a part of this."

We're both trying, and that's all we can do. We both want to build this relationship. We both want to have each other in our lives. The love I have for her is pure and deep, but I'm hurt about how things have happened. Ma has taken it all on board and is working hard to rectify it all. It's a slow process but there's been a lot of progress.

"Mallory Reagan," I hear the nurse call and get to my feet. My stomach starts doing somersaults as I walk toward the nurse. Ma's right behind me. I can feel the warmth of her body against my back. I take a deep breath and smile. Today is the day I'm going to see my baby.

"If you climb up onto the bed, we can take a look for you," the nurse says as we enter the room. It's a dim room with three tiny windows that don't let in much light. The room isn't huge, but it's big enough to fit a bed and a few machines. I climb up onto the bed and Ma takes a seat on the vacant chair beside me. Once again she reaches for my hand, and I don't hesitate to take it, accepting the support she's offering me.

The room is filled with silence as the nurse begins to wave the wand over my stomach. Within seconds, the silence is pierced by a whooshing sound that has my heart swelling with love and pride. Tears fill my eyes as I look at the screen. My baby's on full display. I pull in a sharp breath and watch my baby on the screen. I'm fixated, unable to take my gaze away. God, so beautiful. Nothing, not one thing in this world, is as beautiful or perfect as my baby.

That feeling I had of it not being real has gone. Seeing my baby for the first time is surreal, and the excitement I have for my future is growing every second I stare at his beautiful face on the screen. God, I'm blessed. So damn blessed.

"Everything is measuring as it should do at fourteen weeks," the nurse tells me as she takes the wand away from my stomach. "You're up next to see the midwife to get booked in with your consultant. Any questions or queries you have, she'll be happy to help you with."

I smile at the nurse. "Thank you so much," I say, wishing I had a little more time to look at my baby.

She hands me tissue paper to clean the jelly off my stomach, and Ma quickly helps me clean up. Once I'm ready, the nurse hands me ultrasound pictures of my baby. I beam, unable to keep the smile off my face. God, this day has been amazing.

"Thank you," Ma says as we retake our seats out in the waiting room to wait to be seen by the midwife. "I'm grateful you brought me with you today, Mal."

I rest my head against her shoulder. "I wouldn't have had anyone else with me." Even if Raptor was somehow here, I'd still have Ma with me too.

"You're going to be a great mam, Mallory. You're so loving and caring," she whispers, pressing a kiss to my head. "I love you so very much."

I close my eyes to stop the tears from falling. "I love you too, Ma," I whisper, unable to say anything more as my emotions overwhelm me.

God, this day couldn't get any better.

"Mallory," Chloe cries as I step into the Fury Vipers clubhouse. It's so strange that they have one here in Ireland now, but I'm so very happy for my girl. When I met Raptor that night in New

York, Chloe met Pyro, and they fell madly in love. Pyro was given the opportunity to open a chapter of the Fury Vipers here in Dublin, meaning he could have the club and Chloe. The man didn't hesitate, and with Chloe's family being rich and powerful, it didn't take them long to have everything in order for Pyro to move here. My friend is happy, so very happy. I don't think I've ever seen her like this before, and I'm beyond excited for her new chapter in life.

"Hey," I greet warmly as I step into her embrace. "It's been a while since I've seen you."

I've been hiding. I wanted to take some time to think about what I plan on doing about the baby. I needed to have a clear head and come to a decision I was happy with, one that wasn't influenced by anyone else, and I know if I tell Chloe about the baby then she'll urge me to talk to Raptor and come clean, something I'm still not entirely sure about. I don't want to upend his world. What good will come from me doing that? It's not as though he can move across the world to be here. He lives in New York. His entire life is there.

The gnawing in my gut is back. The guilt I feel lays heavily on my heart. I know he deserves to be told the truth. I just don't want to force him into doing something he never wanted to do. My reasoning is probably selfish, but for now, I'm leaning toward keeping him in the dark. That could change by the time our little one arrives into the world. But as of right now, it's my secret.

"You're not angry, are you?" Chloe questions. "About me giving your number to Raptor?"

"No," I say with a smile. I was at first. I was hurt that she'd done that without speaking to me. But the daily calls and texts I get from Raptor make me smile, and I love that he wants to continue speaking with me. However, with how close we're getting, the secret I carry grows heavier and heavier. I feel like shit for not telling him, but it's what I feel is the right thing to do. "I know you were trying to help."

She grins at me. "Good, because I'm really hoping you two can work things out."

I raise a brow. "How is that going to work exactly?" I ask. "I mean, he's in New York and I'm here in Dublin."

Her grin turns into a beaming smile. "Just have faith," she says as she takes my hand and leads me to a table. "To be honest, I'm just glad James is away from all the bullshit."

My brows knit together. "What's happened?" James is Pyro's real name. She's the only person who calls him that.

"When we were in New York, shit hit the fan. Some of the club girls—"

"And they are?" I ask, wondering what a club girl is.

She pauses, her lips twisting. It's almost if she's contemplating telling me about them. She sighs, releasing a heavy breath. "The club girls are women who enjoy the men. Kind of like rock-star groupies. They're there to have fun and the men enjoy them."

My stomach twists and I swallow back the nausea. "You mean they sleep with them?"

She nods. "It's the way their world is, Mal. It's what they do."

I wave for her to continue, my stomach in knots as I wonder if Raptor is having sex with the club girls in New York. I hate the thought of him with someone else.

"When we were in New York, it came out that some of the club girls were purposefully trying to get pregnant. One woman," she snarls,

"Pepper, managed it. She's pregnant with Preacher's baby. And she's a bitch, Mal. She's such a bitch. I want to rip her hair from her head, she's that fucking awful."

My eyes widen. Chloe isn't someone who speaks badly about people. She grew up with a mam who was rotten to the core, and she was used as a bartering chip against her dad. Thankfully, Chloe met Jess and I around the time she met Callie—who turned out to be the woman her dad was seeing. Her real mam died. Some say Chloe's dad, Denis, got tired of her bullshit and killed her. Others say she was hit by a car and was so badly mangled they had to identify her using dental records. Either way, since she's been gone, Chloe has grown stronger and managed to find who she is without being suffocated or stifled.

"Honestly, Mal, it's fucking despicable," she spits. "Why on earth would anyone trap a man with a baby? Use a damn condom."

My heart sinks. Is that what everyone's going to assume when they find out I'm pregnant—that I trapped Raptor?

Oh my God, they are, especially with what's going on now with the Pepper woman. Jesus, I really have screwed up. There's no way I can tell him now.

Chloe continues to talk about all the shit that's gone on since she's been back in Ireland. She gets daily updates from the old ladies back in New York. Everyone seems really close, and I love that for Chloe. She's happy and thriving, and she looks amazing. Being in love really suits her.

The love she and Pyro share is something I can only dream of. It's not on the cards for me, not anymore. I've got a baby coming and that's what my priority is going to be. Whatever comes after that is a bonus.

"Will you be speaking to Raptor later on?" she asks, pulling me from my thoughts.

I blink. "Probably," I respond. "He'll no doubt text me when he's awake."

He does that every day, but right now, I feel like I have to break ties. I have to stop the communication between us. I hate that I have to do it, but I know it's the only thing I can do. He deserves to have a life, one that's not torn between his duties to his club and brothers, and his child. I wouldn't want him to feel he's obligated to be a father, nor do I want him to feel trapped. I'm scared that I'll be labbled as a baby trapper. I feel so much dread at the thought of Raptor thinking that about me.

I pull in a deep breath, trying my hardest not to cry.

I need to let him go.

CHAPTER 5
RAPTOR

Three Months Later

I hand the stack of cash to the guy who's grinning at me. "They'll be safe," he assures me.

"Of that I have no doubt," I reply, my words laced with a threat. My bike, along with Preacher's, Wrath's, and Pyro's, is all loaded up in a freight container ready to be shipped off to Ireland. It's one of the reasons I've stayed behind a few months. My brothers and I will need our bikes when we're in Ireland, and as Preacher and

Wrath left New York with very little notice, it's been left to me to organize everything.

I should be in Ireland. I need to be there. It's been three months since I've spoken to Mallory; twelve fucking weeks since she returned a call or text. I have no fucking idea what the hell has happened. Pyro told me she's fine and is speaking to Chloe but that whenever my name is mentioned she changes the subject. No one has any clue as to why she stopped responding to me. One minute, everything is fine and we're getting to know one another, the next, it's fucking radio silence. And there's not a fucking thing I can do about it right now as I'm fucking stuck here in New York for a few more weeks. Maybe even longer. The moment my ass lands in Dublin, I'm searching for her. I'm not letting this shit lie. I want to know what the fuck happened.

"You good, brother?" Mayhem questions. He's been sullen as fuck lately. His meddling in shit has led to Preacher leaving and Reaper being pissed. We get why he did it, but fuck, his meddling led to Preach finding out his son isn't his son. In fact, he's his best friend's son. That shit will burn a man. It could break him. For Preach, it hurt him so badly that he had to leave, unable to stand by and watch another man raise the child he thought was his. I'm not sure I could either.

I nod. "All good, though it'll be at least twenty-one days before they arrive in Dublin."

He shakes his head. "Didn't mean about the bikes, brother." He sighs. "I know you're on edge. You want to go as quickly as possible. I get it. If it were Effie, I'd already be on the fuckin' flight. What's goin' on with your woman?"

I run a hand through my hair. "Not a fuckin' clue. She's gone radio silent."

He raises a brow. "What the fuck?" he growls. "You tried callin' her?"

I glare at the asshole. "The fuck do you think?" I snarl. "I texted and called. What else can I do?"

"What's Py said? Has he seen her?"

"No, but Chloe talks to her almost daily. Apparently, whenever I'm mentioned she changes the subject." I'm angry. Beyond fucking angry. What the hell am I supposed to do? I can't be with her. I can't fucking think right now. She's running, and I'm thousands of miles away so I can't fucking chase her.

"Then what's been said to her? Hmm?" he

questions. "A woman doesn't just disappear—unless she's been told somethin'. From what Pyro said, she was at the clubhouse shootin' the shit with Chloe, and then nada, right?"

"You fuckers need to find somethin' else to talk about," I snarl, even more pissed that my brothers are talking about this shit. Fuck.

"Find out what the fuck Chloe and Mallory were talkin' about that day."

"Already done that, brother," I retort. "You think I've been sittin' on my ass the past three months? I spoke to Chloe, and she said they were talkin' about Preacher and Pepper. She explained how the club works—"

"Did Chloe tell her about the club whores?" I watch as his eyes narrow and his lips pull into a scowl.

I still. Every fuckin' part of my body is frozen solid. Fuck, I didn't think of that. "Shit," I snap.

He shakes his head. "If she did, then, brother, you know what the fuck is goin' through your woman's head. She no doubt thinks that while you've been talkin' to her, you've been fuckin' the club whores."

I grit my teeth. "I haven't fuckin' touched any of them." I can't believe I didn't think of this shit before. Christ, I can't even remember the last time I fucked a club whore. It's been months. Hell, maybe even closer to a year. "It all makes fuckin' sense now," I say through clenched teeth. "She probably thinks I've been fuckin' everyone."

He chuckles. "It'll be fine," he says dismissively.

"Yeah?" I growl. "You think a woman who was a virgin when I took her is goin' to think that it's fine when she believes I'm a dog and have been fuckin' anythin' with a pulse?"

"You're goin' to have to let her know that you haven't," he says, backtracking. "I get it, brother; this shit is fucked up, especially when you're across the world from one another. But if you don't find a way to tell her you're not the guy she thinks you are, then when you arrive in Ireland, you're not goin' to find her."

He's right and I fucking hate that shit.

"Look, we've all got your back, brother," he says quietly. "No matter what, we've got your back."

I nod. The gratitude I have for the brotherhood runs as deep as the blood that flows through my veins. "Thanks, brother," I say thickly. "Once I'm back in the clubhouse, I'll call her."

Though I have a feeling she won't pick up. She's been ignoring every call for the past three months. Why would tonight's one make any difference? Either way, I'll be letting her know that the crap about the club girls is fucking bullshit.

"Darlin'," I say with a grin when I see Mallory walking out of Chloe's room in the Gallagher Mansion.

Being in Ireland was only supposed to be for a few days, just until we got this shit with the fucker who had Chloe kidnapped sorted out. But seeing Mallory again makes me want to extend my stay and spend the next few days locked in a room until I've fucked her in every which way possible.

She smiles her soft as fuck smile at me. "Well hey there, stranger. It's been a while."

It's been fucking six weeks since she was in New York, six long fucking weeks. She looks just as beautiful as I remember, even in jeans and a tee. "You doin' good, darlin'?"

She glances around and notices my brothers staring at us, watching our interaction. Fuckers need to get a life. They have their own damn women and should focus on them.

"Why are they watching me?" *she asks, her voice soft as she glances around at my brothers, none of which are making things better. They're gawking at her like they've never seen a woman before.*

"They're assholes," *I snap, glaring at the motherfuckers.* "Ignore them."

Her laughter is soft. "Hard to when they're watching me like vultures. How long are you in town?"

"Not as long as I'd like. Hopin' you'll give me a reason to extend my stay."

Those gorgeous eyes of hers flash with happiness. "Oh, Rap, you're incorrigible."

I chuckle. "You busy?"

She shakes her head. "Not at all. I wanted to see Chloe. She feels overwhelmed right now, so I'm going to leave her be and check in with her tomorrow. What about you?"

"Not in the slightest."

Her smile widens. "Then let's get out of here."

I don't need to be told twice. I take her hand and

lead her out of the Gallagher mansion. I can hear my brothers' laughter following us out.

"You drive?" I ask, wondering how far her house is.

Her brows knit together. "No. But my house isn't far from here. Maybe a fifteen-minute walk."

"Darlin'," I say with a shake of the head. "Seriously?"

She lifts her shoulders and shrugs. "It's not that far."

She's right, it's not. It takes us just over fifteen minutes to walk to her house. The conversation flows between us. Talking with her comes easily, something I struggle to do with other people, my brothers included. But Mallory, she got to me from the get-go. I'm in so fucking deep with her that it fucking scares me.

"Ma's not home. She's away on a work conference," she tells me as she enters the house.

"Which means I can fuck you without worrying someone will walk in?"

Her smile is blinding. "Exactly," she breathes.

I don't hesitate. I close the distance between us, my hand diving into her luscious raven hair. I tug it, pulling her head back so I can kiss her. She gasps against my lips, her hands reaching for my shoulders as our kiss deepens. The air is thick with desire and anticipation. I fucking love the feel of the heat from her body pressed against mine, igniting a fire within me that threatens to consume us both. Christ, I need her. My cock thickens in my pants, straining to be set free.

She moans into my mouth, her tongue dancing with mine as I deepen the kiss. I slide my hand down from her hair, tracing it over her smooth skin until I reach her waist. My fingers hook into the elastic of her skirt, gently pulling it down and revealing the lace of her panties. She whimpers, knowing what's coming next. Fuck, I've missed her.

That's fucked up but it's true. I've missed her and her amazing body.

In one swift movement, I yank her panties down her legs, leaving her completely exposed. She steps out of them and rests her hands on my chest, steadying herself. She looks into my eyes, her gaze filled with fierce desire. I swallow thickly. Christ, I'm close to the edge.

Her hands find their way to my belt, quickly unfastening it and unbuttoning my pants. I watch as she slides them down my legs, revealing my already hard cock. A satisfied grin appears on her face as she reaches out to touch it.

"It's been so long," she whispers, her fingers gently caressing my length.

"Too long," I agree, my voice low and husky.

She licks her lips, her eyes never leaving my erection. Then, with a determined look, she lowers herself until she's on her knees and takes my cock into her mouth. The warmth of her mouth envelops me, her tongue swirling around my shaft as she sucks and strokes me. I groan, my hands threading through her hair as I thrust into her mouth, savoring the sensation.

Her mouth is heaven, and it makes me want to feel her in every possible way. She's driving me to the brink. I fucking love the way her cheeks hollow as she takes my cock deep into her mouth.

I pull back, my breath coming in ragged gasps. *"Enough,"* *I manage to say, even though every fiber in my being is screaming for more. If she continues, I'm going to come, and right now, I want to come while I'm balls deep inside of her.*

She lifts her head, her eyes sparkling with mischief. *"What do you want, then?"* *she asks, tilting her head to the side as she watches me.*

I pull her up into a sitting position, my hands still tangled in her hair. *"Stand up,"* *I command, my voice low and direct.*

She does as I ask, her eyes never leaving mine. I see the desire and fear battling within her, and I know she is mine now. I pull her top off her, my cock thick and hard. I step back, taking a moment to appreciate the sight before me. She stands naked and vulnerable, her raven hair cascading down her back, her eyes full of desire and uncertainty. I want to take her, to fuck her so hard that I'll be permanently etched in her memory.

I move closer to her, my hands reaching out to trace the curves of her body, from the swell of her hips to the delicate line of her collarbone. She shivers under my touch, her eyes never leaving mine, as I continue to explore her.

I grab her hips, my fingers digging into her flesh, and pull her closer to me. Our bodies collide, my erection sliding against her stomach.

"I'm going to fuck you now," I growl, my voice low and gravelly. "And you're going to love every second of it."

She nods, her eyes locked on mine, her breath coming in short, sharp gasps. I bend her over the sofa, her ass in the air. She looks so fucking sexy bent over like this.

I position myself at her entrance, my cock heavy and eager against her. She looks back at me over her shoulder, and I see the fiery desire burning within her eyes.

With a powerful thrust, I enter her, her walls clenching around me like a vice, the sensation overwhelming me. I pull back slightly then thrust again, driving deeper this time, my hips moving in a steady rhythm. She cries out, her hands gripping the corner of the sofa for support as the pleasure coursing through her becomes too much to bear.

Over and over again, I fuck her hard and fast, loving the mewls and gasps that leave her mouth. Her pleas for more are music to my ears. "Raptor, please," she begs.

"Shane," I snarl. "My name is Shane," I say through clenched teeth as I rotate my hips and power into her, my thrusts harder than before.

"Please," she begs.

I pull back again, slowly this time, my eyes never leaving hers. "Say my name," I demand, needing to hear it before I continue.

"Shane," she whispers, her voice shaking with passion.

"That's right," I reply, my voice low and husky. "You're mine now, and I'm going to show you just how much you belong to me."

With that, I thrust forward again, my pace

quickening as I lose myself in her, trying to fight off my impending orgasm. Our moans are mixed with the sound of our flesh slapping against each other. She claws at my arms, her nails digging into my skin, leaving me marked with her desire. I can feel her inner muscles tightening, her orgasm approaching.

"I'm close," she gasps, her voice strained.

"Then come for me," I growl, thrusting harder and faster.

She does as I command, her body trembling as she climaxes around me. I feel her juices coating my cock, her walls clenching and unclenching, milking me of my own release. It's too much, and I can't hold back any longer. With a final, powerful thrust, I release inside her, filling her completely.

I pull out of her slowly, my cock twitching as I collapse to the floor, pulling her down with me.

"Fuck," I snarl. I'm unable to think clearly right now.

"Yeah, that sounds about right," she says with laughter. "Once I'm able to move, I'll order food and then we can go again."

I press a kiss to her head. "That, darlin', sounds like a plan."

I come awake with a gasp. Fuck, it's always

the same dream about her. I spent three days with her when I was in Ireland. I didn't leave her house. She's the only person who knows what my name is; the only one who's ever had the privilege of knowing it.

Mallory is the only woman I want. The moment I'm back in Ireland, I'm going to find out what the fuck happened to her, and from there I can work out a way to fix whatever the fuck happened, because she's still not answering my calls or texts.

Soon, I'll be in Dublin. Then I'm coming for her.

CHAPTER 6
MALLORY

"Mallory," Ma says with a sigh, "you can't stay cooped up inside until you give birth."

Raising the remote, I flick through the channels on the TV, trying to find something I can watch. "Ma, I love you, but I'm not ready to go out."

I feel the sofa dip as she takes a seat beside me; the same sofa that months ago, Raptor fucked me on. My heart races whenever I think about being with him. I miss him. God, I miss him so very much. Not being able to speak to him hurts, and I know I've hurt him by cutting him out of my life. But I had to. I don't want him to think I'm trying to trap him or upend his life.

"Mallory, sweetie, you need to live your life. Why don't you call Jess and see if she's up to going out for lunch? It was her birthday last week, Mal. She hasn't celebrated it," she says with a disapproving tone.

"I know, but you know what her dad's like, Ma," I say softly, hating the shit my best friend has been through. She's been through hell and back and it doesn't seem to have an expiration date. I wish I could take her away from the pain she feels and give her solace, but her dad is a bastard and the threats he's given her are real. There's no way he'd let her go.

"So call her, sweetie; see if she's free."

I sit up, throwing the remote control between Ma and I. "Okay," I say softly as I reach for my cell. "Are you away this weekend?"

She nods. "Unfortunately I am. My flight leaves in five hours, so if you and Jess are going to meet up, let me know and I'll drop you off. I'll leave some money on the side in case you need it."

Disappointment hits me, but I know she has to work. I just wish it didn't take her away. But I'm an adult now and I shouldn't need my mam to hold my hand.

"Listen to me, baby," she says as she kneels in front of me. "I have two months left of traveling, and even with that it's pulled back to once, maybe twice a month. I'm going to be around more, I promise you."

I nod. "I know, and I really appreciate that."

She nods, pressing a kiss to my forehead as she gets to her feet. "Call Jess."

I hit dial on Jess' number and wait as I listen to the ringing.

"Hey, Mal, how are you?" The happiness in her voice has my heart constricting. Damn, I really should spend more time with my friends. I've neglected everyone since I got pregnant. I don't spend enough time with Jess anymore.

"Hey, girl, I'm good. What are you doing today?"

She pauses, and I hear her father talking in the background. "Ma," I say softly, catching her attention before she leaves the room. "Will you speak to Thomas and ask if Jess can stay here?"

Ma doesn't even hesitate. "Of course. If you need me to, I will."

"Thanks." I give her a big grin. "Did you hear that?" I ask Jess.

"I did, and Dad's said yes." She sounds as shocked as I feel. "Is your mam okay to collect me?"

"Absolutely," I reply, watching Ma do a little jig in the corner. "How long do you need?"

Jess laughs. "Ten minutes."

I grin. "We'll be there. I'll text you when we're outside," I promise her.

"Excellent. Thanks, Mal. You're the best. See you soon."

The call ends and Ma's already got her car keys in hand. "Come on, Mal, we'll get you in the car and get Jess."

I smile. My mam is the best. Even though she hasn't really been around, she'll always do whatever it takes to keep me safe, and Jess too. I know I should have told her what has been happening to Jess, she'd have done everything in her power to stop it. But I have to respect Jess' wishes and I regret doing that so much. I wish she can find peace and I know that will only happen if Thomas Grace dies, so I pray for that every single day of my life.

"What's the plan?" I ask. We're currently sitting in a coffee shop. It's been too long since we've hung out and had time for the two of us.

Her father rarely allows her to be with anyone other than me, and with me being so preoccupied with the baby, it's been a rough six months. I wish I was able to be there for her when things are tough.

"I don't know," she replies, reaching for her coffee.

"You didn't get to enjoy your eighteenth like Chloe and I did." I sigh. She was supposed to. Ma even offered to pay for her ticket, as did Chloe's parents, but Thomas put his foot down. The fucking prick was no doubt scared his daughter wouldn't return home if she left to go on a vacation.

"Why don't you go out tonight, let loose and have fun? Your dad isn't in town. You can lie and say you're staying at my house. You'll have so much fun," I say with a grin "Please, Jess. You've been through so much and you never get the chance to let loose and have fun, to be a teenager. You're eighteen now, and I know you're scared of what your father will do, but you have to live once in a while."

When we picked Jess up, she told us her dad is going out of town and that's why he let her stay with us. Either way, I'm glad she's here with me now.

"Earth to Jess." I laugh as I wave my hand in front of her face. She's no doubt daydreaming about Stephen, the guy who's been on her mind since she was fourteen. "Are you listening to me?"

She shakes her head, giving me a soft smile. "Sorry, miles away," she says. "But I think you're right. I should go out and have fun."

My heart gallops at her words, and I can't contain how big my smile is. "Yes," I say a little too loudly. "I'm so proud of you. I have the perfect thing for you to wear."

Jess' back is bad. The scars she has are awful. I should know; I was the one who patched her up and helped her heal from the burns her father gave her.

"Okay. I can't wait to see it," she says, but I see the fear in her eyes. I hate that she's worried, but tonight is all about her and we're going to have the best fun ever.

"I'm so damn proud of you. It's going to be

an amazing night," I promise her. I'll do whatever it takes to ensure it is.

I'M WADDLING through the crowd of people. It's late and I'm tired, but Jess has had the best night ever and I'm not going to be the one to cut it short. I've never seen her so comfortable and at peace before. She let her hair down and had an amazing time. She's buzzed after drinking a few Cosmopolitans. I made sure to not let her get too drunk; just have enough drinks so that she feels the buzz without getting messy.

When I manage to make it outside, the cool air hits me, making me wish I had brought a jacket. I glance around for Jess, knowing she came out here to get some fresh air.

"The fuck are you doing here?" I hear a deep, gravelly voice say.

I turn and see a tall, dark-haired guy towering over Jess. My girl doesn't look scared, and that's because the guy is the dick who's been following her since she was fourteen. Stephen Maguire is a crazy son of a bitch, yet where Jess is concerned it seems as though he has a soft spot. Though looking at the anger in his eyes right now, I'm wondering how true that is.

"Well, it's nice to see you too," Jess retorts, and not that pleasantly.

I grin, proud as hell that my girl is giving as good as she gets. I love that she's not scared around him like she is her father.

"Little Dancer, answer the question. What are you doing here?" he snarls at her.

As much as I feel I should move toward them, I don't. Jess likes Stephen and tonight it's about her. I don't want to get in the way of them.

"I'm having fun. Don't worry, I'm going home now," she tells him with a snap.

The muscle in his cheek twitches. "Who the fuck are you with?"

"My friend. She's in the bathroom," she sighs. "What is your problem?" she asks. "Why are you such an asshole?"

I love that she's not afraid to speak her mind.

"Jessica," he grinds out. "I'm always a fucking asshole. That's never going to change. But why the fuck is your da letting you leave the house looking like that?"

Oh hell fucking no! My girl looks beautiful, and I'll be damned if he makes her feel bad about herself. She's wearing a black jumpsuit and it fits her like a glove, showcasing her curves.

"My dad's not here," Jess replies, unable to keep the hurt from her voice. "You can go, Stephen. I'll be leaving any moment."

That's my cue. I move hurriedly toward them—well, as much as I can in heels at six months pregnant. "Are you ready?" I ask, standing beside her. "Or do you need more time?"

"Not at all," Jess says without looking at the dick who doesn't know when to keep his mouth shut. "Let's go." She links her arm through mine.

She's caught up in her own mind as we walk away from Stephen. She's upset. I know she is. And it's taking everything in her not to cry. I'm trying to keep my anger in check. The last thing Jess needs is for me to lose my shit and give Stephen a piece of my mind. That asshole hurt her with his words and I hate him for doing that.

The streetlights darken and I realize we're away from the busy bars and are walking through a residential area, where a streetlight or two are out.

"Damn," I hear a low growl.

My heart starts to race as I glance at the man who's stepping out of the shadows. He's tall and built like a brick. Fuck... I tighten my arm around Jess. Every scenario is running through my head. What does this man want?

"Where do you think you're going?" the man says as he steps further into the light. Jess and I try to keep on walking. "Hmm? I want to have some fun."

"How about you fuck off before I make you?" I hear the low, growling sound from behind me and quickly glance back to see Stephen striding toward us. I've never seen someone look so frightening before. He looks menacing. "The fuck are you doing here, O'Leary?"

O'Leary? Christ, I didn't think they were in Dublin. From what I heard they were up north, living out of Belfast.

"Well, look who it is. Stephen Maguire, as I live and breathe. What you saying, boss? Do we have a problem?" O'Leary says as he edges closer to Jess and I.

"We'll have more than a problem if you don't leave her alone," Stephen replies, his tone cold and calculating. It's filled with so much anger that Jess flinches.

"Does she mean something to you?" O'Leary asks. "She yours?" he questions as he edges even closer to us. My stomach drops when he reaches out and touches Jess' face.

The next few moments happen in a blur. Stephen rushes forward and starts to punch the guy. "I fucking warned you," Stephen snarls. "Fucking told you to leave her alone."

The sound of flesh hitting flesh has tears falling from my eyes. I'm transfixed as I stare at the scene in front of me. Over and over again Stephen continues to beat the man. My hands instinctively go to my bump as I silently cry. I should help Jess. I should shield her from this. But I'm unable to move. I'm frozen in my spot. She's been through so very much already. Her life has been marred by violence, so this is the last thing she needs. She's stock still in my arms, and I hate that she's in a trance, no doubt regressing into a place she goes when her father lashes out.

Stephen's on top of the man, his fists pounding his face. It's relentless.

"Stop," I shriek as I realize the man isn't moving any longer. "God, will you stop it. Please," I cry, unable to keep the fear from my voice. I'm shaking, absolutely terrified of what's going to happen next.

Thankfully, Stephen listens to my words and stops. My stomach rolls when he stands and I see his fists are covered in blood. God, how deranged must you be to do that—to kill a man with your bare hands in mere minutes?

He glares at Jess and I. "The fuck were you both playing at?" he snarls. "Anything could have happened to either of you."

His words make my anger rise swiftly through my body. How fucking dare he blame this on me and Jess. I want to scream at him; rage that it's his fault, not ours, but I know that won't do anyone any favors. "He's dead," I say softly. "You've killed him."

Stephen shrugs. "Not the first," he says. "He should have listened when I told him to leave Jessica alone."

"Why?" I hiss. God, this man infuriates me like no other. "It's not like Jess is yours. You've made it perfectly clear that she's no one to you. So why are you being such a fucking asshole?" I cry, pissed that he's done this. "Actually, don't answer that. We all know you're crazy as hell. But why don't you just leave Jess alone?"

"Not happening," Stephen growls. "Not fucking happening."

God, he's so fucking annoying. He won't leave her alone but he doesn't want her either. What the hell is wrong with him?

"Come on, Jess," I urge softly. "Let's go home. You're freezing."

"I'll take you," Stephen says thickly. "No fucking arguing. You both need to go home and it's not safe out here."

"I'll call Maverick," Jess says. They're the first words she's spoken since this shit went down. "Besides, you need to sort that out," she tells him, waving her hand in the direction of O'Leary's lifeless body.

"I'll do it," he says, pulling his cell from his pocket and calling his friend Maverick, who is also Jess' cousin.

While he's doing that, I pull Jess into my arms, holding her close. "I'm sorry," I whisper. "I hate that you had to see that. I know it hurts, but you're going to be fine. I promise you, he's not going to hurt you."

She doesn't answer me but she doesn't move from my embrace either. I just want to go home. God, I want to get the fuck out of here and go home where it's safe. I want to talk to Raptor. I need to hear his voice.

I'm terrified there will be retaliation.

I'm so fucking scared that the other O'Learys will come for me, for my baby.

God, what happens next?

CHAPTER 7
RAPTOR

It's been a long-ass day. I've been working on a custom ride for the past nineteen hours and I'm about ready to collapse. I know my brothers are going to want to celebrate that we managed to get the huge fucking order of custom rides done on time, but I'm not wanting that. I'm beyond exhausted. Over the past week, I've barely slept due to trying to get this order ready, but fuck, it's done now and that's the main thing. The money we've made from it is sweet as fuck. Being one of the best custom ride shops on the east coast means we get a fucking lot of business. Every brother has learned the ropes of what to do. Some are better at restoring cars, while others are more experienced at building bikes. When I move to Ireland, I'll be working in the shop there. It's going to take time to build the reputation we have here over there, but we're determined. There's nothing that's going to stop us from becoming the best custom ride shop in Europe too.

My brothers have also opened a strip club that's bringing in a lot of money. We were a little skeptical at first, but the money it's bringing in is worth it. When I get to Ireland, I'll also be working at the club, mainly doing security as that's what's needed. But from what I've heard, it's not that bad. Some of the men used to get a little handsy, but they were kicked out and weren't allowed back. It set a tone, and thankfully, from what Pyro's said, they know better than to do that shit now.

I take the stairs, glad I'm one of the first brothers back at the clubhouse. I need a shower and then I'm sleeping until morning. Before I reach my room, I spot Rush coming out of the kitchen. He's six-foot-three, his hair is shaved, and he's got tattoos on his neck, one of which is his sister's name. Ruby is his world. He'd do anything for her.

"Brother, you good?" Rush asks, his gaze

assessing. He's watching me like a hawk. All the brothers are. They're worried about me, but they shouldn't be. I'm fine—pissed, but fine.

I give him a chin lift. It's fucked to think about how he came to be a brother. The shit he's been through, it would tear a man apart, but Rush, he's doing good. He's got a good head on him. He knows what he did wrong and he's grown to be a man we all respect and are proud to call a brother. Shooting an old lady is something that would usually get you killed, but when Rush shot Octavia he was a punk-ass kid who had no choice. His father was a cunt who had plans to sell his six-year-old sister. Rush did what he had to do in order to save Ruby. It was fucked up that Octavia was caught in the crossfire, but the boy has grown into a man and is loved by the old ladies and respected by the brothers. The past is exactly where it should stay.

"I'm good. Gonna sleep 'til it's next week," I say through a laugh.

"You're gettin' old," he quips. "You're no longer able to keep up with us."

I narrow my eyes, fucking hating that the kid is right. "You wish you could keep up with me, kid, but I wouldn't want to shame you in front of everyone."

His laughter is deep and comes from his belly. The past six months or so, he's gotten better. He's no longer withdrawn or hesitant to be a part of the brotherhood. He's growing into himself, and everyone's fucking happy he is. We were going to drag it out of him, but from what I've seen, Serenity and Esme are the ones who have helped him. Shadow and Reaper's women are sweet as fuck, and they love the kid like he's their own, and we all know that's helped him. He's never had that and those women have given it to him.

"Rap, you want me to send Ruby up to read you a bedtime story?" he asks with a raised brow.

I flip him off. "Fuck off," I hiss as he laughs even harder.

He slaps my back as he passes me. "I'm only joking, Rap. You've worked harder than anyone to get those rides done. Everyone knows that. You worked so our brothers could be with their old ladies and their kids. Go, get some sleep. Maybe tonight's the night you'll talk with Mallory."

I shake my head. That's not going to happen. It's been three months and no fucking word from her. I doubt I'll hear from her until I track her down in Ireland. I don't know what the fuck happened, but I'm going to find out. If something's happened to her, I need to know. But with her speaking with Chloe almost daily, I know that she's alive, which means she just doesn't want to speak with me.

I close my door and start to strip out of my clothes, throwing my wallet, keys, and cell onto the bed. My entire body is fucking tired. There's not a part of me that doesn't feel the exhaustion. Rush was kind of right. I'm thirty-six; I'm getting older. Working over a hundred and thirty hours in a week is taking its toll.

I step into the shower, letting the water cascade onto my shoulders, right where the knots are. Fifteen minutes later, I have a towel wrapped around my waist and I'm exiting the bathroom, when my cell rings. I walk over to the bed and reach for my phone. I'm about to hit ignore when I see the caller ID. Mallory.

It's been three months since I've spoken to her. To have her call me when it's after midnight her time sends chills up my spine.

"Darlin', you okay?" I say as I answer.

I hear a sob break through the line. "Rap," she breathes heavily. "I'm so sorry, I didn't know who else to call. I'm sorry."

I clench my teeth. The sound of her crying is tearing me apart. "Darlin', don't fuckin' apologize for callin' me. What happened? Are you hurt?"

"No, I'm fine. We're fine. I'm just shaken," she continues as she cries. "I just needed to hear your voice."

"Fuck," I snap, pissed that there's over three thousand miles between us. "You sure you're not hurt?" That's what I need to make sure of. If she is, I'll have Pyro at her house within minutes.

"I promise," she sobs, her voice breaking.

"Darlin', I need you to take a deep breath. Can you do that for me?" I say, needing to calm her down before she passes out.

Thankfully, she does as I instruct and I walk her through calming the fuck down. "I'm so sorry," she says once she's got her breathing under control.

"No need to apologize. Tell me what happened." I know if I ask her why she's been ignoring me, she'll either evade the question or end the call.

"I went out with Jess tonight to celebrate her eighteenth," she says softly, hiccupping a little. "We didn't celebrate it when she turned eighteen last week, so I took her out tonight."

"Why didn't you celebrate last week?" I know how tight she is with both Jess and Chloe. She adores both women, so her not celebrating her girl's birthday doesn't sound right.

"Jess' dad is a bastard; a fucking dickhead. The world would be a better place if that man was six-feet under."

I blink at the venom in her voice. Never, not once, have I heard her hate someone, so hearing her talk about her friend's father like that is shocking. "What's the cunt done?" I snarl.

"So much," she breathes. "I wish I could do something to help her, but she won't let me. She's scared her dad will die. I say let him. As for her birthday, he wouldn't let her out, and he sold her car, which she got for her birthday. He's just a bastard."

Sounds like it. "He ever hurt her?"

Silence spreads between us. "Yes," she

admits quietly. "Horrifically," she confesses. "I hate that I haven't been able to tell anyone."

"Why haven't you?" I ask without judgment.

"Her father works for her uncle and cousin. If they find out what that bastard has done to her, they'll kill him, and Jess loves him. He's the only parent she has left and she can't bear the thought of him dying, even if he does deserve it. Jess is the sweetest person you could ever meet. She'd feel as though his death was her fault."

Christ, that's fucked up. "He ever hurt you?"

"No," she says vehemently.

"What happened tonight, darlin'?"

"We left the bar and she got into an argument with Stephen. We started walking away from the bar, intending to go home," she says, and my stomach drops. What the fuck happened and who the hell is Stephen? "We were both so wrapped in our own thoughts we hadn't realized we'd got to an area where some of the streetlights were out. A guy stepped out from the shadows. We had no idea he was there."

"Keep goin', baby. What happened next?" If that cunt touched her, I'm going to kill him. I'll break every fucking bone in his body.

"I don't know. It happened so quickly. One

minute the guy was catcalling, the next, Stephen was there and they were arguing. The guy reached out to touch Jess and Stephen lost his mind. God, Shane, he beat him until he wasn't moving. He killed him."

She begins to sob again and I close my eyes. Fuck, it could have been so fucking much worse had Stephen not been there. God knows what that fucker would have done with two eighteen year olds. Fuck.

"He was just so still. He didn't move," she says, repeating it over and over again. It's as though she's in a trance.

"Baby, listen to me," I say firmly. "Had Stephen not done what he did, that fucker could have hurt you and Jess."

I hear her pull in deep breaths. "I know, but I've never seen anything like that before. I close my eyes and that's all I see. His bloody, lifeless body."

Christ, she's fucking killing me. I hate that I'm here and she's in Ireland. "Those memories will fade, baby," I promise her.

"I'm scared, Rap," she confesses. "I'm so fucking scared that his family will come for me."

My brows knit together. "Talk to me, darlin'. What makes you think that?"

"He killed Jarlath O'Leary, Rap, the son of the gangster Fintan O'Leary. They're animals, so bad that they fled Dublin and relocated to Belfast. His dad's not going to let this slide. I was there, Rap. I watched his son die. Why would he let me live?"

The sobs start once again, and I can't deny that her words make sense. Fuck, my stomach is twisted and acid burns deep. "It's going to be okay," I tell her, though that's not something I can promise her. "I'll have Pyro check in on you."

"No," she shouts. "No, I'll be fine. I don't need help. I just wanted to talk. I'm sorry, I shouldn't have called. Don't call Pyro. I'm fine." The finality in her tone pisses me off. She's scared, fucking terrified, so why won't she let me have Pyro help her?

"Mal, you've got to fuckin' talk to me. What's goin' on?"

"Nothing," she lies.

"Bullshit. Three months I haven't heard from you. What the fuck? What happened?"

I hear her heavy sigh. "You live in New York, Raptor. I live in Dublin. My life is here and yours is there. Why are we wasting time? What could ever come from this? It's best we just sever ties and leave it as it is."

"You think that's what I want? I know it's not what you want." She's not good at telling lies. Her accent thickens and her voice raises an octave. "So how about we try again? What the hell is going on?"

"I won't destroy your life. I won't trap you into this. Please, Rap, just leave it be."

"Listen to me, darlin', in fifteen weeks, my ass is back in Ireland. I'll be coming for you."

I hear her heavy sigh. "You said that before," she snaps. "I'm not putting my life on hold, Raptor. It's not fair to ask me to do that. It's not right to expect that of me."

"You find someone else?" I growl. The mere thought of her with someone else makes me homicidal.

"No," she shrieks. "God, what do you take me for? You're an ass, Raptor. But I refuse to live in limbo as you decide when you're actually coming for a visit." I hear the sound of a car door slam. "Ma's home. I'll be okay. I'm really sorry for calling you. I hope you have a good night."

"Told you already," I snarl, pissed that she's

trying to brush me off, "I'm glad you called, and don't apologize. I've been losin' my fuckin' mind tryin' to figure out what the fuck is goin' on with you. Thought you were hurt or somethin' as you've been ignorin' my calls and texts. But I get it. You're pissed that I haven't been back to see you. Well, I promise you, Mal, fifteen weeks and I'll be there." I wish it were sooner, but we've got another thirty customs to build before I leave and there's no fucking way I can leave my brothers to deal with that alone.

"You know what, Rap, I'll believe it when I see it. Be safe," she whispers as she ends the call.

I stare down at my cell and wonder what the fuck I'm going to do now. I want Py to check in on her, but I know that'll just make things between us even worse. Christ, I'm so fucking torn.

Just over three months and I'll be in Ireland, and when I get there, I'm coming for her.

CHAPTER 8
MALLORY

"How are you doing?" Jess asks as we sit in the waiting area.

Today is my scan day and I've finally, finally decided to find out what the gender of my baby is. I have been thinking long and hard about what's going to happen since the call with Raptor last week. He seemed pretty adamant that he'd be here in just over three months, and if he is, I'll tell him about the baby. I'll have given birth by then.

"I'm doing okay. How about you?" I ask, reaching for her hand.

"The nightmares are still here, but I'm hoping they'll go soon."

I nod. "Me too," I whisper.

The nightmares are horrendous. The sound of Stephen beating Jarlath repeats over and over again. It's terrifying. Not to mention the fear of Fintan finding out that I was there the night his son died. Jess' dad works for Jerry Houlihan, the head of the Houlihan gang. There's no way Fintan would come for her, nor would he go after Stephen. I'm the only one who has no ties to a criminal enterprise, and that's what scares me the most.

"Where's your mam?" Jess questions, glancing around the waiting area for the fourth time since we arrived. I'm not sure if it's in search of Ma, who should be here, or if it's the fear from the night last week.

"She's running late," I tell her with a sigh. "She's been working away and was due back this morning."

Ma promised she'd be here for the scan and I had no reason to not believe her. She's been present so much throughout my pregnancy so far. I'm a little saddened that today—the day we find out the gender—is the day she's late. I'm trying my hardest not to let it get to me, nor am I going to hold it against her. Things like this happen, especially when it's out of our control, and Ma's job is out of my control. So I'm taking deep breaths and praying that she'll make it, especially as my appointment is running late too.

"She'll be here," she assures me. "Your mam knows that she deeply hurt you when you were growing up. She's not going to let you down. Have faith."

Jess continues to amaze me every day. She's been through so very much and yet she has the best and most positive outlook on everything.

"How are things between you and Stephen?" I ask, wondering if she's going to talk to me about him. Over the past week, we've checked in daily but she's not mentioned Stephen at all.

She lifts her shoulders and shrugs. "Eh, I haven't heard from him since that night. But it's okay. That's what Stephen does best. He pops up into my life, makes me feel so many things, and then disappears."

I hate that he does that. He gets her hopes up that there could be more between them and then pulls the rug from under her when he walks away without a second glance.

"What about Maverick?" I ask. Her cousin has been a lot more present lately, which I love.

"I think having him around more has Dad backing off me. It wouldn't look good if I had bruises. Maverick would instantly know what's happened."

I harrumph. "The bastard's too damn sly. He damn well knows what he's doing. I really wish Maverick would find out. He'd kill your dad and we can all be happier."

Jess shakes her head. "I love you, Mallory."

I rest my head on her shoulder. "I love you too."

The swish of the doors opening has my gaze moving toward the woman hurrying toward us. "I'm so sorry I'm late. Have you been seen yet?"

"Ma, calm down," I say as I take in her red, blotchy face and panicked expression. "The nurse is running late. You're on time."

The beaming smile she gives me makes my heart fill with love and warmth. "Thank God for that," she says, blowing out a heavy breath. "Jessica love, how are you?"

Jess gets to her feet and hugs Ma. "I'm good, Jayne, thanks."

"So what are we thinking?" Ma asks. "Boy or girl?"

"Either," I reply, laying my hand on my ever-growing bump. "Healthy."

Ma nods, pride shining in her eyes. "You're going to make an amazing ma, Mallory. I'm so very proud of you."

I shake my hand at her. "Don't you dare make me cry," I hiss as tears sting the backs of my eyes.

Jess laughs. "I have a feeling that Mal's having a boy."

Ma nods in agreement. "I do too. Either way, boy or girl, they'll be loved dearly."

I swallow hard. She's right, my baby is going to be so loved. I can't wait to meet him or her. I just hate that Raptor won't know about the baby. I don't want to tell him over the phone. It's a life changing moment and doing it when he's thousands of miles away from us isn't the best way to do it. If he's not here in fifteen weeks, then I'll tell him. Until then, I'm going to continue as things have been.

"Miss Reagan?" the nurse calls out, and I rise to my feet. "Hello, Mallory, how are you feeling?" she asks once we're in the room.

"Good; a lot more energetic than I was at the beginning of the pregnancy."

She smiles. "Are the baby's movements frequent?"

I nod. "Yep, especially first thing in the morning. I swear, one of these days I'm going to end up wetting the bed when the baby kicks my bladder."

Ma laughs. "I remember those days."

"If you can lift your top, we'll be able to get a good look at the baby."

I lie back on the bed, lifting the hem of my t-shirt over my bump and holding it there. I wince as the cold jelly hits my stomach. "Sorry," the nurse says sheepishly as she begins to scan along my belly.

The sound of my baby's heartbeat fills the air and I'm fixated on the screen, watching as my baby moves.

"He's a kicker, that's for sure," the nurse says, and I gasp at her words. She smiles brightly as she waves the wand over my boy. "Congratulations, Mallory, you're having a boy. The measurements are right on track for this stage of the pregnancy."

I'm unable to keep the smile from my face. God, I'm so damn happy. I never knew this type of happiness could exist. I'm already so in love with my son. I have no idea how that's possible, but it's true.

The nurse continues to take measurements and I turn to see Ma smiling, her eyes filled with tears as she watches her grandson on the screen. Jess has her cell out and is taking pictures, something I should have thought to do, but I'm grateful that she has done so.

"All done. As I said, everything seems to be on track. You know the drill: anything—and I mean anything at all—feels off, you come straight up to the maternity ward. Don't wait around. It's always best to be safe." She hands me some ultrasound pictures, all while smiling. I can't imagine how rewarding this job is, to let parents know about their babies. Although it must be devastating to deliver the worst news possible to expectant parents.

"Thank you so much," I say as I try to get off the bed. Ma reaches out and helps me off. "Have a wonderful day."

"You too," the nurse replies as she opens the door for us to leave.

"I knew it." Jess claps as we exit the hospital. "I knew it was a boy."

Ma laughs. "Any ideas on a name yet, Mal?"

I nod. "I've been thinking about this for a long time and I've decided on Shay."

Both Jess and Ma beam. "I love it," Ma says softly. "I think it's perfect."

"Me too," Jess whispers. "I'm so very proud of you, Mal, Your mam's right, you're going to be the best mam ever. Maverick's here now to collect me, but I'll call you tomorrow and we'll set up a coffee date?"

I pull her into my arms, holding her tight. "Definitely," I promise her.

We walk her to Maverick's car and watch as they drive away. I'm glad she has Maverick to protect her now. I feel a little better about her leaving these days. I just pray that she's going to find a way to escape.

"We're going shopping," Ma tells me as she links her arm through mine. "We've got things to purchase before the little man arrives."

I laugh. She's so giddy and I love that.

I GLANCE at the car behind us. It's been on our tail for at least forty minutes and it's making me paranoid. I see the northern registration on the car and begin to breathe deeply. It can't be. Can it?

"Mallory, what's wrong?" Ma asks as we stop at a traffic light. "Sweetie, what's going on? You look like you've seen a ghost."

"Ma, is that one of the O'Learys behind us?" I ask, my voice shaking. I have a tight grip on the door handle.

Ma looks in the rearview mirror, her eyes squinting as she concentrates. "Yes, that's Micah. Why?"

My entire body begins to tremble and I feel as though I'm about to throw up. God, this can't be happening.

"Mallory, sweetie, I need you to tell me what's happened."

Before I'm able to speak, the car behind us moves to the left of us. He's right by my window, a sinister grin on his face. I watch in horror as he slowly runs his thumb along his throat. It's a clear threat. God, he's going to kill me.

Ma drives off, running the red light. "Ma," I cry.

"No," she says, her voice hard. "That man has just threatened you. How do you know him?"

I'm still trembling. God, I didn't want this to happen. I had hoped it wouldn't, but it has.

I tell Ma everything that happened last week. Everything that's happened to Jess spews out of me like word vomit. I just can't keep it in.

"Why didn't you tell me any of this? God, poor Jess. How the hell was that man allowed to hurt her?"

"You can't tell anyone, Ma. Please," I urge her, knowing how hurt Jess would be knowing it was me who spilled my guts.

"I won't, but if anything else happens to her, I won't keep quiet. Do you understand?"

I nod, grateful she's given me that. "What about Micah?"

Her lips twist into a snarl. "We can't stay at the house any longer, Mal. He'll know where we live. I won't take any chances right now. The moment we're home, we have thirty minutes. Grab whatever you need, anything important, and then we're leaving. Do you understand?"

I nod, confused by how direct she's being. It's almost as though she's been waiting for something like this to happen.

"Sweetie, your father was part of the Kelly's organization. I've always wondered if something could happen to us. I've always had an exit strategy. Everyone needs one."

I'm in shock. Confused and hurt. She's never said that about my dad before.

"He was a bastard," she hisses. "He was close to Sean Kelly Senior, love, and he was cheating with any woman who gave him the time of day."

I shake my head. "Why didn't you tell me?"

She reaches across and grabs my hand. "I didn't want you to hate him as I had done."

"Where is he?" I ask, wondering if he's close by.

"I don't know. I lost track of him when you were eight. I haven't heard from him since then."

"He could be dead then?"

She's silent, and I know that means yes.

"Where will we go?" I ask, wondering if we're leaving Dublin.

"Let me worry about that. You focus on you and Shay. I have everything else under control."

I nod, grateful she's here. I'm not sure what would have happened if she weren't.

God, I'm terrified. Micah isn't going to stop. He's out for blood. I just pray that he doesn't get it.

CHAPTER 9
RAPTOR

"Yo, Raptor," Prez calls as I enter the kitchen. "You busy, brother?"

I shake my head. "Not right now," I tell him. I'll be heading to the custom ride shop soon. There are a couple of bikes that need to be finished before the big order begins.

"Good. I need you to get your shit together. Your flight leaves in a few hours."

I blink. "What?" The fuck is he talking about? What flight? Where the hell am I flying to?

"Brother, your flight to Ireland leaves in a few hours. You've got to get your stuff. I ain't shippin' that over."

I laugh at his words. "Funny, Prez, but I ain't goin' anywhere yet. We've got custom rides that need to be finished before the big order begins. I ain't leavin' you short."

He shakes his head. "You won't be. We've got it covered. Rush and Cage finished those customs last night. They've both learned from the best. You. So they're more than capable of takin' over from you when the order starts. So pack your bags, brother. You're goin' to Ireland."

I stare at the man who's not only my president, but my brother, a friend. "You serious?" I ask, my heart racing. Fuck... Can it be true? Am I actually heading for Dublin?

"Deadly. Now don't take this to mean we don't want you here. You're goin' to be a tough act to follow, brother, but you're needed with Py, Wrath, and Preach. They've done well recruitin' but they're nowhere near where they need to be. We all know your mind is in Dublin, on Mallory. So, brother, go find your woman and tie her to the fuckin' bed," he says with a laugh while shaking his head. "That woman blows hot and cold, but I get it. Long distance ain't for everyone. Now, you don't have to be. Just make sure she's worth it."

He has no fucking idea just how worth it Mallory truly is. The woman is all I fucking think about. She's still not answering her calls or texts. I haven't spoken to her since the night she called. But she's doing okay. Pyro's keeping an eye on her through Chloe. They haven't seen her in months but have spoken to her daily. She's alive and doing okay, according to Chloe. I'll feel better once I'm in Dublin and can see for myself.

"Best get to packin', brother. You haven't got long and there's no fuckin' way you're leavin' without saying goodbye to everyone. So you'd best get to it."

I shake my head, still trying to wrap my head around this shit. "This your idea?" I ask.

"Not entirely. I think Rush was the mastermind behind it all. That fucker's been workin' his ass off."

That's for sure. While I've been working on customs for the past few months, I've had both Rush and Cage with me, teaching them the ropes. They're both fast learners and now they're able to build bikes themselves, and they're fucking good at it. Leaving New York, I'll know that I won't be leaving my brothers in the lurch. They've got Rush and Cage to help out when things get busy. Both boys are going to make the Vipers a lot of fucking money.

"Go," Ace urges. "Get your stuff packed and then say goodbye to the women."

I laugh. I know the women are going to cry. They've been a part of the club for years, and I've helped each of them throughout that time. They're like sisters to me. Saying goodbye ain't going to be easy, but what I have waiting for me in Dublin is going to be more than fucking worth it.

I don't hang around. I head to my bedroom, surprised to find Rush standing by my door. "You good, brother?" I ask.

He nods, a big old smile on his face. "I'm good. Wanted to see if you needed a hand."

I open my door and he follows in behind me. "I appreciate everythin' you're doin', Rush."

"Your woman means the world to you, Rap. I've seen how the brothers are with their women and yours is halfway across the world. It's got to be fuckin' hard. You've been wantin' to be with her for months and it just seemed as though everythin' kept getting piled on and you couldn't leave."

Gratitude hits me hard. Fuck, he's one hell of a brother. "Gotta say, man, words can't describe how much I'm in your debt."

He shakes his head. "I'm repayin' my own, Rap. When I was released from juvie, it was you who kept me on the straight and narrow. Unlike the other brothers, who watched me like a hawk and kept waitin' on me to fuck up, you were at my side, showin' me the ropes, keepin' me on the right path. You knew what I needed to succeed. I'll never forget what you've done for me, brother," he says thickly. "From the bottom of my heart, Rap, I owe you my life. If it weren't for you, I'm not sure if I would have been able to succeed."

I reach for him and pull him into me. He doesn't tense. Instead, he returns the hug. "Trust me, kid, if there's anyone in this world who would have been able to right the wrongs they've done and find the right path to continue on, it's you. No one fuckin' blames you for what went down when you were a child. You had no choice, and while your actions hurt someone we all care about, they also led to Ruby being saved. Trust me, brother, you belong here."

"As annoyin' as you are," he says as he pulls back from me, "I'll miss you, old man."

I chuckle. "I would invite you to come with me but I doubt you'd leave Ruby behind."

I see something whirring behind his eyes. "I've thought about it."

Now that's something I hadn't expected. "And?"

"It's a fuckin' lot to leave behind. My sister, Cage, Seri and Esme."

It's telling that he hasn't said Digger and Octavia. While they took him in, they haven't treated him as they have done Ruby and it's obviously weighed heavily on Rush.

"It's a decision only you can make. If it's one you want to make, you'll have to be prepared for the guilt trips."

He laughs. "Yeah, no doubt."

I study him. "You want the move, don't you?"

He glances away. "Here, I'm always goin' to be the punk kid who shot Octavia. The only ones who don't treat me that way are you, Pyro, and Wrath."

Fuck, the kid's struggling. "You want me to speak with Ace?"

He shakes his head. "I've already spoken with him. He's spoken with Pyro and he's agreed. It's just a club vote now, brother."

I laugh. "Fucker. You had me thinkin' you were stayin' here."

He grins. "What do you think's goin' to happen when the women find out I'm goin'?"

"Hence the guilt trips." It won't just be Ruby, but Seri and Esme. Probably Octavia too.

"I know that if I stay here I'm not goin' to shake that tag, brother, but my hands are tied unless the club votes it."

"They will. Don't worry, they'll know that this is what you want. Havin' you in Dublin will help a fuckin' lot to grow the club."

He grins. "What do you need help with?" he asks, glancing around my room.

"Nothin'. I just need to pack my clothes. Everythin' else is just crap I don't need."

He nods. "I get it. When you have no family other than the brothers, you don't tend to have much. It was the same with Preach when he upped and left."

"The same when you do too."

He lifts his shoulders and shrugs. "We'll see."

I give it six months and he'll be in Dublin with us. If I have my way it'll be a fucking lot sooner than that too. "It also makes sense as to why you're puttin' in all the overtime."

He chuckles. "That helps, but I want a new bike. Mine is good, but it's not me."

"Trust me, kid, I get that. You ever need help, I'm only a call away."

He reaches out to shake my hand and I pull him in for one last hug. "Get your woman, Rap. I can't wait to meet her."

This kid is the fucking shit. "Be good, kid. I'll see you soon."

He leaves my room and I begin to pack my clothes. I know the goodbyes are going to be long, and I appreciate Rush taking the time to say his privately.

"Brother," Pyro greets as I exit the airport. "It's about fuckin' time."

I chuckle. Getting off the plane, it felt as though I was home. Everything in me settled the second I breathed in the Irish air. "Tell me about it. How is everyone?"

"Good. You'll see for yourself that life here isn't as hectic as it was back in the States. Even Preacher is doin' better."

I nod, glad my brother is doing okay. His world turned upside down when he found out Tyson wasn't his son. It fucked him up mentally and it's got to be hard to come back from that.

"Ace said you spoke to Rush. What do you think about havin' him here?" he questions as we climb into the SUV.

"I think it will be a huge benefit to us to have him here. He's a good kid. He'll thrive here."

He grins. "That's exactly what I said to Ace when he spoke to me about it. Havin' Rush here will boost our numbers. Not only that, but it'll give us a better in with the younger generation. So far we've only got Tank and Bozo who are under the age of twenty-five."

Tank and Bozo are the prospects for the Dublin chapter. From what I understand, they'll make great additions to the club.

"When Dig and Octavia find out, they'll lose their minds," I tell him. "I'm surprised they haven't known he's wanted to leave. It's clear he's not entirely comfortable with them. He's a lot closer to Esme and Serenity, and in turn Shadow and Reaper."

"It's got to be hard for them, Dig especially. Tavia was hurt because of Rush's actions. He's got to live with the reminder that his woman was shot for the rest of his life. It's got to be even harder knowing the boy who shot her is livin' in the same clubhouse."

"When you put it that way..." I muse. But it's still fucked up that even after all these years they've never let him close, and that's why he wants to leave. He's a good kid and can feel the disconnect from them. Leaving will make Dig and Octavia better, and it'll give Rush a fresh start. "When will the vote be?"

"We're havin' ours tomorrow, and from what Ace said, tomorrow evening is when they'll have theirs."

"He'll get the votes," I say adamantly.

"No doubt. I've given Wrath and Preach the head's up about it, and from what I've gotten from them, they're both willing to vote in favor of Rush moving."

I take a deep breath. I just hope the other brothers are the same and vote for him to move.

"Now, you've not asked about her, but I know you're dyin' to know. Brother, Chloe's not heard from her at all for the past forty-eight hours. All calls and texts are goin' straight to voicemail. Jess said she spoke to her yesterday but hasn't spoken to her today, and like Chloe, her calls are goin' to voicemail."

My gut tightens. Fuck. What the hell?

"I'm takin' you to her home now. I know you don't want to wait. I wouldn't if it were Chloe."

The rest of the drive is tense. I'm on edge as Pyro drives us, my mind fucking racing as I think about what the fuck could have happened.

It takes close to thirty minutes before we reach Mallory's house. It brings back memories of when I was last here. Christ, it's been too fucking long.

"Brother," Pyro says low, "the door's ajar."

Just as we reach the door, it's opened and a tall, dark-haired guy walks out, his head held high, his gaze on us. It's clear this man is a killer. "Pyro," he greets.

"Rap, brother, this is Maverick, Chloe's uncle and Jessica's cousin."

I give him a chin lift as he smiles at me. "Jess told me what happened and asked me to check it out. The house is empty. They left in a hurry, taking only half their clothes, both Mallory and Jayne's. We'll find out where they've gone."

"Their cell phones?" I rasp.

"Sitting on the kitchen table. I assure you, we're going to find them. But from what it looks like, they've upped and left willingly." He turns to Pyro. "If I have news, I'll have Jess call Chloe."

Py nods. "Appreciate it, Mav. Thanks."

I watch as Maverick leaves, a sickening feeling in my gut. Something's happened. I just know it has. I shouldn't have left it this long to come here. I should have trusted my gut when she stopped taking my calls.

Now I have to find her. I won't stop until I do.

CHAPTER 10
MALLORY

Three Months Later

I wince as another pain rips through me. God, did it have to be today? I'm in labor. There's no question about it. My contractions have been happening on and off all day, and they're getting more intense as the day wears on, not to mention they're happening more frequently too. I reach for my cell and hit dial on Ma's number. For the past three months, she's been working from the office only once a week, ensuring she's home with me the majority of the time. Today, of course, had to be the day she's in the office, and she's not called me back despite the thirty missed calls she's had from me.

That night when Micah made his threat to me, Ma packed us up and moved us to the outskirts of Dublin. With a city with over a million people, it was easy enough for us to hide. Thankfully, Micah hasn't made an appearance since that night, and I know that's down to Ma hiding us. She's extremely careful to ensure that she's not followed when coming home from work or the grocery store. She's doing everything she can to ensure our safety and I love her so much for doing that.

"Ugh," I groan through the contraction. "Ma, please... God, please answer the damn phone."

I'm not going to be able to drive myself to the hospital and there's no way an ambulance will get to me in time. God, I really need my mam. Once again the phone goes to voicemail, and I'm left wondering what the hell I'm going to do. There's no way in hell I'm going to give birth at home. I'm scared enough as it is. I won't—can't do this alone.

I decide to do something I promised myself I wouldn't do. I call Jess, knowing Micah could be watching, which means she could end up being caught in this mess. Either way, I have no choice. She's my only option right now. I'm just praying she'll answer.

"Hello?" I hear her soft voice say, and I sob in relief. "Mallory?"

"Hey," I whisper, letting her know it's me. "Sorry, I didn't mean to scare you."

"What's wrong?" she asks. "Is everything okay?"

"Not really. Ma's at work and I'm in labor. I need to get to the hospital but my contractions are coming quickly. I won't be able to drive myself."

"I'm on the way," she assures me. I can hear her walking. "Mav's let me use his car if I need it. So far, I haven't needed to, but today I will. Are you okay?"

"Yeah," I say, grateful that I have her to talk to. "Are you sure you're okay to come?"

I hear her little laugh. "There's nowhere else in this world that I'd rather be. I'm in the car now and I'm coming."

Relief washes through me. God, what did I do to deserve a friend like her?

"I'll call you when I'm outside. Do you have everything packed?"

"Yes," I breathe. "I have the bag by the door waiting. I'm ready to go."

"Excellent," she cries. "I'll be there soon. Are you still staying in the same house?"

"Yeah, we're still here."

Jess has no idea why Ma and I left the house in the city and moved to the outskirts. She had Maverick check in on me and they discovered the house was empty after Ma and I left. We'd left our cells there in case Micah was tracking them. Thankfully, Jess hasn't really questioned it. I told her that Ma wanted to move due to it being better for the baby and the house having an office for her to work out of.

"See you soon. Today's the day we get to meet Shay."

My heart's racing, but the joy that fills it with her words is overwhelming. Yes, today is the day we get to meet my son. This is the day I've been looking forward to for so long. It's kind of hard to imagine that it's finally here. But I'm excited to meet him. We're all calling him Shay, and it's something that I love. I've known since the moment I found out I was having a boy what I wanted to name him. I wanted to name him after his father, Shane.

"I'm hanging up now, but I won't be long."

"Thank you. Drive safely," I urge as we end the call.

My cell starts to ring the moment my call with Jess finishes. Relief unlike any other hits me when I see Ma's name flashing on the screen.

"Ma," I answer. "Finally. God, are you okay?"

"I'm so sorry, love. I've been in meetings all day. Is it time?"

She doesn't need to be told. She already knows. "Yes. I'm sorry for all the calls."

"Hush, sweetie, it's okay. I'm on my way home. How are you doing?"

I cry. "I'm scared. I didn't think you'd make it. I've called Jess. She's also on her way."

"I would have always made it, Mallory. I wouldn't have missed this for the world. I'm about fifteen minutes from home. When I called, you were on another call so I left work instantly. I shouldn't be too long. Just let me know if you're not okay."

"I'm fine, Ma. I promise. Just scared and overwhelmed."

"That's to be expected. I'll be home soon. Love you, sweetie."

I close my eyes and let her words sink over me. "I love you too. Drive safe."

I waddle over to the front door, putting my cell into my bag so that it's ready for when I leave. My stomach tightens, and within seconds, a huge pop sounds, followed by a loud, gushing sound. Shit, my waters have just broken.

I glance down at the puddle at my feet and wonder why the midwife lied to me. She told me it wouldn't be a big gush like in the movies, rather just a small trickle. I call bullshit because right now I'm standing in what's akin to the bloody river Liffey.

Thankfully, I'm able to clean up the mess and my feet, but I don't have time to change. A car is pulling up out front. I peer through the window and see it's Ma's car that's parked out front. She doesn't turn off the engine. Instead, she slides out of the front seat and races toward the house. "Mallory, are you okay?" she asks as she opens the front door.

"Yeah. I have some towels to put on the seat. My water has broken," I tell her, breathing hard as I waddle toward her. "I don't want to ruin your seats."

Ma smiles at me, pulling me into her arms. "It's okay. The interior can be washed. Are you ready?"

I nod. "Ready as I'll ever be. Is Jess here yet?"

"She parked out front while I parked in the drive. Let me help you into the car," she says softly as she takes my arm and leads me out of the house, stopping to pick up my hospital bag on the way out.

I get into the car and smile when I see Jess is already sitting in the seat beside me. She helps me to put on the seatbelt. "You're not alone."

I grin. "No. I should have never panicked," I say with a laugh. "But damn, Ma left it late."

Jess giggles. "She wanted to make you sweat. Jayne always loves to be the drama."

"I do not," Ma says from the front seat as she drives out of the driveway. "But either way, today is the day. I'm going to be a granny. I'm so damn excited."

Jess nods. "I'm going to be an auntie. I can't believe it's finally here. How are you feeling, Mal? Stressed, excited, overwhelmed?"

"Before I called you, I was all three. Now I'm excited, scared, nervous, and overwhelmed. The stress has gone now that you're both here with me." Before I can thank her, a contraction rips through me and steals my breath away. I try to breathe through it, trying my hardest not to scream out loud, knowing Ma will be upset and worried if I do. Instead, I bite my lip and try to breathe through my nose.

"That's it," Jess encourages me. "Like that, deep breaths. In and out. Breathe through it."

I glance at her, wondering where the hell she learned that.

She gives me a sheepish smile. "Um, I may have been taking online Lamaze classes in case you needed me."

"Oh Jess," I whisper, completely blown away by her. "You're amazing."

She lifts her shoulders and shrugs. "Hardly. You'd do the same for me. In fact, you've done a lot more," she says softly so only I can hear her. "You're my best friend. We're closer than sisters. I'm here for you whenever you need me, just as I know that you are when the tables are turned. It's going to be okay."

Jess holds my hand as Ma drives us to the hospital. The contractions are now every four minutes, as timed by Jess. The fear that I had is intensifying as the pain of the contractions gets worse. Holy hell, how do people do this more than once? I'm about ready to lie down and call it a night. It's bloody sore.

"You're doing amazing, Mallory. Honest, you're so damn brilliant," Jess praises, and I want to cry at the pride in her voice.

"Ma, how much longer?" I ask through gritted teeth.

"We should be at the hospital in ten minutes or so depending on traffic."

I let out a harsh breath. Damn it, that's not what I meant.

"Um, Jayne, I'm pretty sure Mal meant how long until she has the baby?" Jess clarifies for me.

"How am I to know?" Ma asks as she stops at a red light. She turns to face me. "Sweetie, everyone is different. This is your first baby and it could take a while."

I shake my head. "It hurts," I tell her. "It's only going to get worse. I don't want to do this anymore."

Jess' fingers brush over my hair. "You're

doing amazingly. We'll be at the hospital soon and we can get you the good drugs."

I sigh as I turn to her. "Promise?"

Jess laughs and nods furiously. "Promise. There'll be something you can take that'll help ease the pain, right, Jayne?"

"Oh yeah. When I had you, I had all the good stuff. It'll depend on how far you're dilated to see what we can get you."

"Everything," I hiss as yet another contraction hits me. "It seems quicker than four minutes," I yell as the pain once again takes my breath away.

"That's because it is," Jess says, still running her fingers over my hair. "There's two minutes."

"Ma," I cry, horrified. "Please don't let me give birth in the back of your car."

I can hear the laughter in her voice. "Don't worry, love, you won't. We'll be there soon."

"If all else fails, keep your legs closed. That should stop the baby coming, right?" Jess asks, glancing between Ma and I.

"Don't think it works like that, Jess," I say, trying to catch my breath. "The baby comes when it wants. We have no say over the matter."

"It'll be okay," she promises me as she continues to try and help me relax.

"We're here," Ma says as she parks in front of the hospital. "Jess, run in and grab a wheelchair. There's no way Mallory will be able to walk. Once you have that, you take her to the maternity ward and I'll park the car." Ma's all business, and I'm so damn grateful that she is. She's taking charge and leading the way. I don't have the capacity to do that right now. I'm in pain and I'm exhausted. The contractions have been coming since around ten a.m. this morning and it's almost six in the evening. I just want this over with and then I can have my little boy in my arms.

It doesn't take Jess long to have a wheelchair ready for me. With the help of her and Ma, I'm out of the car and sitting in the chair with my bag on my lap. I grip hold of the arms of the chair as yet another damned contraction racks through me. Ma presses a kiss to my head. "I'll be as quick as I can," she promises me.

I don't want her to go, but I know she has to park the car. She climbs into the driver's seat and pulls away from the curb. I watch as she drives away from the entrance and toward the car park.

"Ready?" Jess asks once my contraction is finished.

"Yeah," I say, my voice a little wobbly. I'm wondering just how the hell I'm supposed to give birth when it's so damn painful already. I know everyone has a different pain threshold, but mine must be nonexistent. I've never had to deal with physical pain. I had no idea what to think going into this. Ma tried to forewarn me about the pain, but nothing could have prepared me for this.

We get to the maternity floor and it seems as though it's all hands on deck.

"Mallory," my midwife, Claire, says as she gets me situated on the bed. "We just need to see how far you're dilated."

I nod. My hand is tight in Jess' grip. My girl isn't letting go of me. I'm so damn grateful she's here.

"She's in pain," Jess tells her. "Is there anything you can give her when the contractions hit?"

The midwife checks me out. "I'm sorry, but we'll only be able to offer gas and air at this time. Mallory's close to ten centimeters dilated, which means she's too far along for an epidural."

"Give me anything," I cry as another contraction hits.

I hear Claire laugh as she sets me up with the gas and air machine. She walks me through how to use it, and the moment I inhale deeply, I feel as though I'm floating. It doesn't take all the pain away, but it makes it bearable. The door opens to my room and Ma walks in. I sob. I'm so glad she's here that I actually begin to sob.

"It's okay," she promises me as she comes to stand by my side. "You're almost there."

"She's almost ten centimeters dilated," Jess informs her.

"Yes," Claire says with a smile. "Are you all ready?"

I nod. I'm more than ready for this.

Seventy-five minutes later, I have a beautiful baby boy in my arms. There may have been a lot of curse words and threats made to Raptor's appendage while I was in the throes of labor, but now that I'm holding my baby in my arms, I feel so content. God, I can't believe I'm a mam now.

"Wow," Jess says in awe. "That was beautiful. Thank you for letting me be a part of it. I'm so in love with my nephew."

"I wouldn't have had it any other way," I assure her. "Thank you for being here with us."

I glance down at my son, who's fast asleep against my chest, and know I'll do whatever it takes to protect him from anything that threatens to harm him.

CHAPTER 11
MALLORY

I'm exhausted. Every piece of my body feels tired. But looking at Shay, I can't help but be grateful that I feel that way. I love my son, and it's hard to believe that he's finally here. It's been almost twenty-four hours since he was born and we're being discharged. I get to take him home with me and I'm so damn excited. Ma's taken time off work to spend with us and help me if I need it. I also love that she gets that time to bond with Shay also.

"You ready?" Ma asks as she comes to stand next to me. She's been really good. She's not taken over like I thought she may have. Instead, she's standing back and following my lead. I struggled with breastfeeding, and instead of letting me wallow in self-pity at failing, she told me about how she, too, couldn't get into it and that as long as the baby is fed, that's all that's important.

"Yeah. Is he strapped in okay?" I ask, looking at Shay in his car seat.

"Mallory," she whispers, placing her arm around my shoulders, "the midwife checked and assured you he is. He's perfectly strapped in. You're doing great. Don't doubt yourself."

This is why she's the shit. She's so supportive. I wish I had spoken to her years ago about the neglect that I had felt due to her working all the time. Had I done, maybe things would have been different a while ago. But I'm glad that she's here and we've been able to grow our relationship. I have no doubt that she's going to be the best granny ever.

It takes a while longer before we're discharged, and the moment I'm in the car with Shay strapped in beside me, I feel at ease. I can't wait to be home with him and just take the time to bond.

"You hungry, love?" Ma asks. "I can stop off at McDonald's drive thru, if you'd like."

I groan in happiness. "Yes, please."

Ma laughs. "Okay. Same as usual?"

"Like you have to ask."

Ma orders me a chicken burger, fries, and a chocolate milkshake, while she has a beef burger, fries, and a diet coke. Shay's fast asleep. He seems to like the car. Within minutes of Ma driving, he was drifting off. I tuck into the food, my gaze focused on my boy, who's snoring softly. I wonder if he could get any cuter. He's got dark hair that covers the majority of his head. Ma and the midwife told me it could fall out as he gets older but not to worry as it'll grow back.

"Is there anything you need before we go home?" Ma asks as she nears the edge of the city.

"I don't think so, do I?"

She laughs softly. "We'll do an inventory when we get home. I think we may need to get some formula. The little you have will probably only last through the night.

"Oh, and probably some more nappies," I groan as I lean my head back against the rest.

"Don't worry. Once you're home and settled, I'll run to the shop and get the bits we need until it's time to do the full shop. That gives us a little time to think if we need anything else."

I continue to eat as Ma talks about getting a photo shoot done for newborns, and while it sounds amazing, I have to make a call first. It's time for Raptor to know he has a son. It's going to be a hard conversation, and I have no doubt that he'll be mad, but I did what I thought was best. Though now I'm regretting it. I should have told him from the get-go. He deserved to be with me at the hospital. I hate that I've not let him have that experience, and I understand if he never wants to speak to me again. I just pray that he'll want to know his son.

We arrive home and Ma helps me out of the car and carries a sleeping Shay into the house. I manage to get him out of the car seat and into the crib without waking him.

I lie down on the bed beside the crib and watch him sleep. He's so peaceful. I love watching him sleep. I adore that contented sigh he gives when he's snoring. I reach for my cell and search through the contacts, the ones I saved before I left my original cell at our home. I hit call on the number, my heart racing, my stomach clenching. God, I hope he answers. I really hope he does.

"We're sorry; you have reached a number

that has been disconnected or is no longer in service."

My heart shatters at the message. Why isn't his number in service? Crap. What have I done?

Tears gather in my eyes and I shut them tight, not wanting them to fall. Damn it. Why did I push him away? I turn over and cry softly into my pillow, careful not to make too much noise and wake Shay. I feel heartbroken. I feel as though I've lost Raptor, and I have no one to blame but myself. Had I been open and honest with him from the beginning, we may not be in this mess.

God, I'm such a bitch. I fucked up. Majorly. I just pray there's a way to fix it.

A WEIRD SENSATION falls over me and I wake with a start. My eyes adjust to the darkness, and my heart starts to race as I see a tall figure standing over me. He's right beside Shay's crib. I swallow back a scream as I feel the sharp edge of a knife at my throat.

"I know who you are." I hear the thickness of his voice. "Mallory Reagan, I've been watching you. Waiting for the right moment to get my revenge."

I stare into the white orbs of the man's eyes, and I know instantly who it is. Micah O'Leary. "What?" I breathe.

"You were there," he snarls, his breath hot against my face, the knife pressing deeper against my throat. "You watched as my brother was murdered, and you did nothing. You just stood back and watched that animal kill him."

"What could I do?" I ask, my entire body trembling with fear. "What should I have done?"

I froze that night. I was rooted to the spot and I froze. There was nothing I could have done other than try to pull Stephen away from him. But Stephen outweighs me and is a hell of a lot taller than me. What would have happened had I tried to intervene?

"You did nothing," he snarls. "Not a fucking thing. And because of that, we had to bury my brother."

I hate that he's angry. I completely understand his anger, but there was nothing I could have done. I was never going to help. Stephen was always going to kill Jarlath for touching Jess and nothing anyone did would have stopped it. Nothing.

"He's dead, and it's because of you and that bastard Maguire. I'm going to enjoy toying with you."

His knife slices through the skin at the base of my neck, and then he drags the blade down to my chest. I whimper, tears falling thick and fast. My mind is focused on making sure that he doesn't get to Shay. I can't—won't let him hurt my baby. I'll endure anything if it means he'll stay the hell away from my son.

The knife gets deeper as he slices through my shirt and into the skin on my chest, before pulling the knife down to my arm. I feel my blood soaking through my clothes and onto the bed beneath me. "Stop," I plead, my voice coming out in a hiss.

"You never said that to Maguire, not until it was too late," he growls as he continues to slice along my skin. "I'm going to break you, Mallory. I'm going to ensure that you're a sobbing mess before I kill you. You can call it karma for what you've done."

"Nothing," I cry. "I did nothing."

He lifts off me, the knife moves away, and I'm

able to take a deep breath. The pain from the cuts is painful, but I'm so focused on him that I push it from my mind. I need to keep my focus elsewhere, otherwise I'll lose it.

"Exactly," he sneers. "You did nothing."

I hear Ma's bedroom door open, and I watch as Micah gets a sinister smile on his face. "I'll be seeing you soon, Mallory. I'd keep one eye open at all times."

He thrusts the knife into my stomach, and just as quickly as he stabbed me, he withdraws the blade and rushes from the room. I'm in shock, unable to move as blood pours from my wound like a fucking river. I slap my hand over the wound to try to stop the blood, but it's no use. The liquid gushes through my fingers.

"What are you doing here?" Ma screams. "Mallory? Mallory?"

She rushes into my room, flicking on the light. She releases a horrified cry as she moves toward me. "Oh Mallory," she cries. "It's going to be okay. I promise it'll be okay. I'll get you to a hospital."

I shake my head. "No, we have to leave. He'll come for us," I say through ragged breathing. "He's nowhere near finished with me, Ma."

She's sobbing as she tries to help me stop the bleeding. Shay's cries fill the room.

"Ma, help Shay," I whisper as my body begins to sink into the darkness. "No hospital, Ma."

"No hospital, baby," she cries. "I'm going to get help, okay?"

I nod, praying she'll take care of Shay as I'm pulled into the abyss.

CHAPTER 12
RAPTOR

FIFTEEN WEEKS LATER

"Brother, you good?" Wrath asks as he slides a beer over to me. "You've been sitting here for the past thirty minutes. What's up?"

"Nothin'," I say as I reach for the beer and take a sip.

"Bullshit, Rap. You've been fuckin' down for months. Is it the woman?"

"Don't," I say through clenched teeth. This isn't the first time one of my brothers has told me to forget her. I've had the majority of them say it. Pyro and Rush haven't. They both know what Mallory means to me. It's fucked up that it's been six months since I arrived in Ireland, six fucking months, and I've not heard a fucking peep about where she is.

"Brother, it's been months—"

I spear him with a glare. "Don't," I warn once again. "Don't fuckin' go there, Wrath. Not ever."

He holds his hands up and sighs. "Okay. So what's the plan then?"

"Just like that?" I ask, wondering why he's changing his tune.

"Just like that," he confirms. "I've known you a long time, Rap. You've never been like this over a woman. So yeah, it's that simple. So what's the plan?"

I don't fucking know. "I have Freddie searching for her. The last two times he had a lead, he missed her by days. I'm telling you, brother, I know she's in trouble. The way she's movin', not stayin' too long, always in different places, it's like she's on the run."

"What's Chloe and Jess said?" he asks, his gaze intense.

I'm just fucking relieved that he's not pushing that 'leave her be' bullshit.

"They talk to her. It's a very quick check in, according to Chloe. Jess is currently in hidin', from what Maverick has said, and that's not to be repeated to anyone. Chloe doesn't know."

His brows knit together. "Py thinks that's wise?"

I nod. "After the shit Chloe went through when she was kidnapped, she still has nightmares. The shit Jess has been through will trigger her. Jess has been tortured, from what Maverick's said. He's keeping me updated on what Jess is saying about Mallory."

He nods. "Then, brother, it's time to pass a message along to Jess. Let her know that you're in town and looking for Mallory. Why not cut the middle man? We both know Jess won't keep that to herself. From what I'm gettin' from this, Mallory and Jess are thick as thieves. I'm reckonin' Jess knows a lot more than she's lettin' on. What do you think?"

"Yeah, but the woman is holed up with Stephen Maguire, Wrath. What do you think 'the Eraser' is goin' to do if I push back against his woman?"

"I'd think that a man who's woman's been tortured would know what it feels like to know your woman's on the run and hidin'. Surely he'd be receptive to findin' out information for us?"

"I have Freddie on it. I'll talk to Maverick and have him ask her to let Mallory know that I'm in town. If that fails, then we'll go to Stephen."

Wrath nods. "Good. We'll find her, Rap. We're goin' to fuckin' find her. Have no doubt about that."

I just hope that I find her in time. Things around here have been crazy. Preach found his woman, Ailbhe. She's pregnant with his kid, not to mention taking care of her siblings. Of course, when Preacher found out she was pregnant, he lost his shit and was an ass. He flew back to New York, and while he was there, his woman got worked over. Thankfully, that bastard was dealt with and Preacher is doing a lot fucking better. He's no longer living in the past, worried about what could happen. He's present for Ailbhe and her siblings.

"The question, brother, is what condition is she goin' to be in when we do find her?"

His silence is more than enough for me. Yeah, shit's going down with Mallory. I know it is. I'm fucking worried that she could be dead before I find her.

I just need to see her, make sure she's doing okay. That's all I fucking want.

Christ, I'm losing my damn mind. I can't focus. I can't do shit but worry about my woman.

I'M STANDING at the door of the strip club. I'm working the door. It's a Saturday night and the drunks are out looking for a good time. It's almost closing, and Bozo's inside with Tank, making sure the women are safe while I'm out here.

Over the past six months, I've come to know the new patched members. They're great additions to the club. Bozo is smart as a whip. The fucker could be a rocket scientist if he wanted. Tank is quiet and sullen, but he's not a dick about it. Then there's Cowboy. He's quick to smile and quick to flirt; a real charmer all the women love, including the club whores. The other new member is Hustler. The name speaks for itself. He was on the verge of going to prison for his schemes. The fucker can't go a day without trying to hustle someone.

When Rush arrives, he'll fit in nicely. The vote happened the day after I arrived in Dublin and it was unanimously voted for. Rush will soon be a member of the Fury Vipers Dublin chapter. That's not to say that there wasn't anger at his decision, especially from Digger. He was shocked when he found out Rush wanted to leave. But Ace set him straight, and in turn the shit died down. Rush is due out here any day now, and the brothers here are excited.

"Raptor, just the man I'm looking for." I hear a thick Dublin accent and turn to my right to see Freddie Kinnock striding toward me. "Your woman knows you're in town. Let me just say, I've never seen a woman smile as widely as Mallory did when she learned that tidbit. I reckon you have about twenty-four hours before she tracks you down. Good luck, man, you're in for a treat." He doesn't hang around and wait for me to speak. He turns on his heel while laughing away to himself.

My heart races. Fuck. Could it be true? Is she finally coming around?

I guess tomorrow will bring the answers.

CHAPTER 13
MALLORY

"Hey, sweetie, you doing okay?" Ma asks as she places a cup of tea on my desk. "You've barely slept."

I glance at her. She's worried. I get it. Whenever we leave the house, we're on edge, wondering when Micah's going to show his face. Over the past three months, he's found me on four separate occasions. Each time he finds me, he beats me until I'm on the verge of unconsciousness and then flees. In the past three months I've had a broken nose, broken arm, and a broken leg, not to mention I've been stabbed on multiple occasions. Micah wasn't lying when he told me he was going to break me. I'm so fucking frightened to leave the house, scared that he's right behind me, ready to attack when he feels like it.

"I'm okay, Ma, just been busy." It's not a lie. With Ma working from home, she's not able to earn as much as she used to, and with three mouths to feed now, along with having to save money away for a rainy day, things have become tight. I began looking for a job not long after Shay was born, and I found one. It suits me perfectly. I can work from home and work around Ma and Shay.

"This job," she says as she takes a seat on the bed, her voice soft so as not to wake Shay, who's sleeping soundly in his crib. "Are you sure it's safe?"

I glance at my son. His face is content as he sleeps. It's hard to believe he's three months old now. The time has gone by so fast. He's growing like a weed.

"Ma, right now it's paying the bills, and that's all that matters. No one knows my identity other than the owner and she's not going to say anything. I'm helping her out by taking these tasks off her hands."

She sighs heavily. "You're organizing hits, Mallory. It's not an easy job nor is it safe."

"I know," I whisper, hating that this was the only job I could get. "Ma, your life has been turned upside down because of me. The job you love isn't there anymore because you've had to step back to protect me. I'm doing what I can to ensure that we're all doing okay. If it means sending messages to people I don't know with details for their target, then so be it. I don't know these people and I would like to keep it that way."

She reaches for my arm. "I hate that you have to do this in the first place."

I squeeze her hand. "It gives me time to spend with Shay. Watching him grow up and getting to be here is everything I could have wanted. This job may not be for everyone, but Ma, the shit we've been through the last three months, it's made me not feel for this job. I'm good at keeping it separate from my real life."

"I'm proud of you, love. You're doing amazing, even if we are in hiding. Are you sure you're good to go tomorrow? I don't want anything to happen to you."

I smile. Tomorrow, my best friend is getting married, and I wouldn't miss it for the world. She's finally getting her happy ever after and I'm thrilled for her. I always knew she and Stephen would end up together. He was the only person she was interested in, ever since she was fourteen. It's always been him. I'm just thankful he got his head out of his ass and saw that she's his. I'll always have love for Stephen. He's saved her. Her father is still alive but he's in hiding. I know that once Stephen finds him, he's going to kill him, and the day that happens I'm going to celebrate by dancing on the fucker's grave.

"Yes, I'm sure. I would never miss Jess' wedding, Mam. I'd love it if you and Shay could come, but we know that's not safe. Right now, this home is secure, and as long as only one of us leave, Shay will remain safe. I can't have him or you hurt, Ma, not for me. I'd never forgive myself."

She gives me a sad smile. "I know, sweetie. I just wish things were different. Have you tried calling Shay's dad again?"

Sadness hits me deep in the pit of my stomach. "Yeah," I whisper. The same thing happens every time I call the number. It's no longer in use. I've no way of contacting him, and I've not spoken to Chloe in a while, not wanting to bring my shit to her doorstep. She's been through enough as it is. So we text a lot. I've asked her about Raptor via text but she never replied, and I got the feeling she didn't want to talk to me about it as she changed the subject quickly, so I dropped it.

"Honey, maybe one day you'll find out how to get a hold of him."

I nod. "I'm thinking of asking my boss," I say softly. "She's amazing at locating people. I know it would cost me, but I think it'll be worth it."

Ma smiles. "I think so too. Now, get some rest. You've been awake all night. If Shay wakes up, I'll take care of him. It's been a while since I've had some snuggles with the little guy."

"Okay, Ma. Thanks."

She gets to her feet and presses a kiss to my forehead. "I love you, Mallory. Get some rest." She walks out of my room and I do as she says. I climb into bed and lie down, my gaze on Shay, who's fast asleep. He only wakes once at night for a feed and that's usually around midnight. He won't wake again until about six or seven. Today, it's the latter.

I close my eyes, and it doesn't take long until I'm drifting off.

I HELP Jess fix her veil as she stares at herself in the mirror. "How?" she asks, her eyes filling with tears.

When I got the phone call three days ago to tell me that Jess was getting married, I was shocked but excited. Then Jer and Stephen demanded help with everything. They want today to be special for Jess, and I adore them so very much for that.

"Stephen and Jerry both wanted you to have a wedding dress, Jess. They wanted this day to be special for you. They called me and asked me to pick a dress you'd love. They wanted to surprise you. I'm so happy you love it." I grin at her as I explain the calls I received. "I have to admit, I was shocked when I heard you were getting married, but who you were getting married to didn't surprise me."

Her laughter is soft and melodical. It's been a long time since I've heard her laugh so carefree. "It's always been Stephen."

I nod. Anyone could see that. "It really has. I'm glad he got his head out of his ass and has also stopped stalking you. I'm even more grateful that he saved you. I'm sorry I couldn't."

Jess shakes her head, her eyes filled with horror. "No," she whispers as tears shine in her eyes. "You were my rock, Mal. You've always been my rock. Where's my handsome nephew?"

I glance away, hating that I couldn't bring him with me. The guilt that I have is real. I feel so much guilt for having to hide him away from the world because of the shit I'm in.

"Mal," Jess whispers. "What's going on?"

I blink away the tears. I will not cry. This is her day. I'm not ruining it. "It's fine. You're getting married today. That's a joyous occasion."

"No," she says adamantly, reaching out and gripping my hands. "Mallory, what's going on? Talk to me, please."

I can't help but clutch on to them, scared that if I tell her, things will get worse. "I'm in trouble," I whisper. "God, Jess, I'm so scared."

"What's happened?" she asks, her eyes wide and her lips parted.

"The night that we went out before Shay was born," I say low, hoping no one is listening. "Remember what happened?"

She nods. It's not every day you watch

someone beat another man to death. It's ingrained in our minds. Neither of us will ever forget what happened.

"The O'Learys aren't happy, Jess," I tell her, hating that I'm doing this today of all days. "Micah O'Leary has been trailing me."

She blinks, her brow furrowed. "What?" she hisses harshly. "Mallory, why did you never tell me?"

"You've been going through so much, I couldn't tell you. I didn't want you to live in fear either."

Jess shakes her head. "God, Mallory, you should have told me. I would have helped you. What's he done?" she questions. She knows me too well. "Tell me, please. What's he done to you?"

I glance away, taking a steadying breath. "Please," I beg, my voice just above a whisper. "This is your wedding day, Jess. Please just leave it be."

"Tell me," she urges. "Please."

"He threatened to kill us, Jess. Threatened Shay and me. He broke into our home and held a knife to my throat while Shay was lying in his crib beside me. I was so scared," I cry, my tears coming thick and fast. "Ma came home and he ran away. Since then, we've been in hiding. I hate that I'm so scared. I'm afraid that he'll find me."

I don't delve into everything else that's happened. She doesn't need to know all the gory details. My dress hides the scars Micah has given me, and I'm glad that it does. Otherwise she'd be in tears at the sight of them.

"I'm so sorry," she whispers softly. The pain in her eyes makes my stomach clench. God, this isn't her fault. It's not.

"It's not your fault, Jess," I tell her as I swipe away my tears. "This isn't on you. This is on them. They're doing this, not you. We'll be fine."

"I'll talk with Uncle Jer, Maverick, and Stephen. We'll make sure this stops. God, Mal, I'm so very sorry. I should have known something was wrong. I'm so sorry."

I pull her into my arms. I hate that I've made her sad on her wedding day, but I'm so damn glad I've told her the truth. "Don't apologize. I haven't told anyone. I'm so scared, Jess, so damn scared. What if he gets to Shay?"

"We'll make you safe," she promises me.

"I know," I reply softly. If anyone can it will be Jess. She'll do whatever she can. "Ma's been a

Godsend, Jess. She's finally present and here. She dotes on Shay and she's finally showing me that she cares." I love how much Ma has changed. We're getting along so great, and I know it's not for show. She's deeply sorry for neglecting me emotionally as a child and she won't do it again.

"I'm glad she's around more and that she's present, watching Shay grow up. Nothing will happen to any of you. I'll talk to Maverick and Jer today," she says with a grin, her eyes filled with grit and determination. "They'll help."

I can't help but smile. Maybe, just maybe, things are looking up. "I know. I love you."

"With my entire heart," she replies.

God, she's killing me. I swipe away the tears once again and take a deep breath. "Let's get you married."

Watching Stephen watch Jess as she walks down the aisle toward him makes me so happy. The love he has for her is so very clear to see. I had that. Looking back, I see that's exactly the way Raptor would look at me. God, I really did fuck up with all of that. I wish there was an undo button and I could fix everything.

I'm smiling wide and bright throughout the entire ceremony. Jess and Stephen love each other, there's no denying that, and together they look perfect. They've been dancing around one another for years. It's finally time they were together. I couldn't be happier for Jess. She deserves this and so very much more.

"I now pronounce you husband and wife. You may kiss the bride," the officiant says, and I laugh as Stephen slides his arms around Jess' waist and hauls her close to him. The kiss is something that looks like it came from a movie. The two of them are caught up in one another, just the way it should be.

"Mallory." I hear the deep south Dublin accent and turn to see Freddie Kinnock standing beside me. "You're a hard woman to track down."

I raise a brow. "Oh, you've been looking for me?" I ask, and I'm shocked when he nods. "Why?"

"A guy's been looking for you for close to six months."

My heart starts to race and my body feels weak. God, no.

"You've got the attention of the American. He's been looking for you for a long time," he continues.

His words filter through my panic. "What?" I croak, trying to regain my breath.

"Raptor," he says evenly. "He's in Dublin, been living here for the past six months."

"What?" I breathe. "He's here?"

He frowns. "You didn't know?"

I shake my head. "No, I've been hiding."

His eyes narrow. "Why?"

"Micah O'Leary found out I was there that night," I confess softly, knowing Jess is going to tell Stephen and Jer anyway. It's only a matter of time before they tell Freddie.

"Christ, that fucker. What's he done?"

I shake my head. "Where is Raptor?"

"At the Fury Vipers clubhouse," he says. "But don't think you're going to get away without telling me what the fuck's going on. Mallory, what the hell has that cunt done to you?"

I once again shake my head. "I don't want Jess to know," I tell him quietly. "She feels guilty enough as it is. Me and my baby are in hiding so he doesn't find us, Freddie. The day I came home from the hospital with Shay, that animal broke into our home."

His nostrils flare. "What did he do?"

I pull the neckline of my dress down a little,

showing him part of the scar I have. "He threatened me; held a knife to my throat while my son lay asleep in the crib beside me. He sliced me open and stabbed me. He blames me for what happened to his brother."

His jaw clenches. "He'll not hurt you again."

I give him a sad smile. "He's in hiding, Freddie. Over the past three months, he's found me four times. The man isn't going to stop until he kills me."

He pulls me into his arms. "Trust me," he says thickly, "he's not going to fucking touch you again."

I don't respond. He has no way of knowing that. There's no way in hell he can assure me of that. I can't trust anyone but myself to keep my son safe.

Tomorrow, I'll see Raptor. Maybe, just maybe, he'll be able to help keep Shay and Ma safe.

CHAPTER 14
MALLORY

It's almost midnight and the party is finally over. Stephen and Jess left a little while ago, while Jer, Maverick, and Freddie decided to enjoy the festivities and drink more alcohol than necessary.

"Mav, Freddie, do either of you need a lift home?" I ask as I reach for my cell.

I had planned on going home when Stephen and Jess left, but Ma persuaded me to stay a little longer. She's enjoying having the house to herself—what she actually means is that she likes the alone time with Shay. As I know my son is safe, I stayed. Now, I'm wanting to go home, snuggle with my son, and go to sleep. Tomorrow is going to be an emotionally charged day and there's no way I can do it without getting some sleep.

I'm worried about what Raptor's going to say. He's going to be angry. I get that and I'm expecting it. I fucked up, majorly, by not telling him about Shay, but I'm hoping he'll be interested in getting to know his son.

"Yes," Mav slurs. "Although, we should be the ones bringing you home," he says as he gets to his feet. "Why didn't you tell any of us what the fuck was happening?"

I shrug, feeling self conscious. "I didn't tell anyone."

"Stupid," Freddie says as he downs the last of his whiskey. "So stupid."

"Shut up, Freddie," Maverick hisses, before turning back to me. "You should have told Jess or Chloe. They'd have told us and we'd have helped."

"Both Chloe and Jess have been through enough pain and suffering. Telling them about me would only add to it. So no, neither of them are ever going to know the full extent of what's going on."

"You women," Jer says, shaking his head.

"You need to tell us when you're in danger. How the fuck are we supposed to help?"

"I'm in danger because Stephen killed a man. Want to tell me how the fuck that's fair?" I ask, my anger getting the best of me right now. "How is it fair that I'm the one who's been targeted? I have a three-month-old son who can't leave the house because I'm terrified Micah's going to hurt him."

Silence spreads around the room, and I know they finally understand why I've been hiding. Maverick pulls me into a hug. "The next time that fucker surfaces, you call us, Mal. You call any of us and we'll be there."

"Exactly," Jer says. "Now, why don't you move in here?" he asks. "You'll be safe. The house is guarded and no one can get in or out without my say so."

"Tomorrow, I'm going to the Fury Viper compound. If Raptor won't help with Shay, then I may take you up on that offer."

"Wait," Maverick says, his eyes widening. "Raptor's Shay's dad?"

I nod. "He is."

"Fuck me," Mav says. "That's news to me. What the hell is with the women in my life?" he muses. "None of you can go for guys your own age."

I laugh because he's not wrong. His sister, Callie, is married to a man twenty years her senior. There's about an eight or nine year difference between Pyro and Chloe. With Stephen and Jess, there's around a fifteen year age gap. Raptor is thirty-five and I'm nineteen. "We'll see what you're like when you meet your woman."

His gaze slides to the floor, making me think he's already found his one. I'm happy for him if he has. Maverick is one of the good ones.

"Okay, you two, let's go. I'll get you home," I say, walking over to Jer and pressing a kiss to his cheek. "Thank you for having me today and including me in the planning."

He pats my hand. "My dear, if it wasn't for you, my niece wouldn't have had her dream day. You're the reason she's alive and happy. We're in your debt."

I shake my head. "No, you're not. Jess is closer to me than a sister. I'll do anything for her." I give him a smile before turning and leaving. It's time to go home and I can't wait. I'm about ready to drop.

Thankfully, both Maverick and Freddie dutifully follow me to my car.

I drop Freddie in town. I'm not sure what he wants to do, but I know better than to ask, whereas Maverick wants to be dropped off at home. I happily oblige, knowing they're safe. Once I have them dropped off, I call Ma.

"Hey, sweetie, are you on the way home?"

"Yeah. I just wanted to know if you need anything?"

I hear her soft yawn and realize I've probably woken her up. "No thanks, love. I'm going up to bed now. Shay's all tucked in and fast asleep."

I smile. He's safe and content. "Okay. I'm going to stop and get some food. I'm hungry. I'll be home in a bit. I'll be sure to be quiet so as not to wake anyone."

"Thanks, Mallory. I'm glad you had a great night. I can't wait to hear all about it tomorrow."

"Night, Ma. Sweet dreams." I end the call and continue driving.

I stop off at a fast food restaurant and get some food before I go home.

I'm careful to keep an eye on any cars on the road. Micah has been showing up out of nowhere. It's as though he's got a tracker on me or something, but I've changed vehicles and have checked to ensure there are no trackers. Yet somehow he always manages to find me.

I pull into the car park of the fast food chain and quickly make my way into the store. I'm cautious, my gaze always scanning to see who's around me. Thankfully it's quiet and hardly anyone's around, so I'm able to order my food and get it within minutes.

Walking outside, I sigh when I see a huge fucking truck blocking my exit. The fucker is parked vertically, blocking the view between the store and my car. Fuck. I hurry around the truck and hit the key fob of my car to unlock it. I see the lights flash and it beeps, letting me know it's unlocked. My feet hurry toward my car. My entire body is tense as fear creeps up my spine. I'm trying my hardest to not panic. Christ, what the hell is wrong with this asshole? Why would he park like this, blocking a car in?

I reach for the handle to open the door and the hairs on the back of my neck stand up. "Told you, bitch," I hear snarled from behind me.

I begin to tremble. Fuck, fuck, I should have known. I should have walked back into the store and waited. I shouldn't have walked into the dark car park alone. How fucking stupid am I? Us women, we learn this as we grow up. Never walk alone at night, always have your keys between your fingers—just in case. If you have to be alone, always call someone to talk to and let them know your whereabouts so if something does happen to you, they can get help.

What do I do? Ignore every instinct I have and walk toward danger. Christ, what the fuck is wrong with me?

I drop the food I was carrying to the floor with a loud thud, and my car keys clink as they fall out of my pocket. I turn to face Micah, my heart pounding. Even though I know what's coming, his sinister smile sends chills down my spine. "Micah," I breathe, fear coating every syllable.

He holds up his trusted knife again, the blade glinting menacingly in the dim light. "Warned you, bitch," he spits, his eyes filled with malice. "I told you I'm going to break you, Mallory. I'm going to toy with you until you beg for mercy."

But I refuse to give him that satisfaction. No matter what he does to me, I will not beg for mercy. I did nothing wrong. I couldn't have stopped them that night. Stephen was protecting the woman he loves from Jarlath's cruel intentions. The man is a psychopath, and there was no stopping him when he set out for revenge. In the three months since he broke into my house the day I came home with Shay, I've replayed it over and over in my mind. And now I realize that no matter what actions I could have taken, Stephen was always going to kill Jarlath. It's just who he is.

"Karma has come back around," Micah growls.

"I did nothing wrong," I cry out as he lunges toward me, his knife piercing through my stomach.

"Exactly," he hisses as he kicks at my legs, sending me crashing to the ground in pain. Blood seeps from my stomach wound, staining my clothes and the ground beneath me. "You did nothing, you fucking bitch. Not a damn thing." The pain is excruciating, but I refuse to give him the satisfaction of seeing me suffer.

He unleashes a relentless attack, each kick more powerful than the last. His blows land all over my body, leaving me unable to defend myself. He's like a force of nature, too strong for me to resist. "Please, stop," I plead, gasping for air.

"Never," he snarls, his voice dripping with malice. "This is only the beginning." He laughs maniacally as he grabs my arm and yanks it backwards. A sharp pain shoots through my body as something pops out of place. But he doesn't stop there. With a ferocious growl, he launches himself at me, raining his fists down on my face and chest. I try to fight back, to shake him off, but his strength is overwhelming. Every blow feels like a hammer striking against my skin.

Can this really be happening? Why am I being punished for something I didn't do? I close my eyes, my heart feeling like it's about to burst from my chest. There's no way out of this nightmare.

Micah's hands tighten around my neck, and my vision begins to blur as I struggle to stay conscious. I think he may just kill me this time.

As Micah releases my neck, I try to pull myself together, to find the strength to break free from his grip. But it's no use. He's way too powerful. I try to call out for help, but my voice is gone, silenced by his savage attack.

My body jolts as a rush of air hits me, and the crushing weight on my chest is lifted. I lift my head, watching him sprint toward the truck. My heart begins to race with fear as I wonder what his next move will be. I can't stay here. What if he comes back?

My arm that he pulled is useless. I can't move it. If I try to, it radiates with pain. With my good hand, I scan around the floor, trying to locate my keys, my gaze firmly on Micah, who's watching me from his truck. My heart is beating so fast, I'm scared I'm going to pass out.

"Ah," I cry when my fingers curl around my keys. I've found them. God, I've found them.

It takes everything I have to lift myself from the ground and open the car door. I won't fail. I will not let that monster win. I throw myself into the car and lock the doors. The second I hear the lock engage, I begin to sob. Every inch of my body is in pain and I'm struggling to breathe, yet all I can do is sob. Tears fall thick and fast as I try to catch my breath, but it's no use. The pain I'm in is taking my breath from me. There's no escaping it.

I hear a heavy engine sound and see Micah reversing the truck from the car park. Relief hits me, but it's short-lived as the pain hits me. He's leaving. God, he's leaving. A rush of breath leaves me and once again my vision starts to blur. This time, I'm unable to fight the darkness. It pulls me under and I welcome it.

I WAKE TO PAIN, and I blink harshly at the sunlight that's beaming through my window. Fuck. What time is it?

I try to reach for my cell but my arm protests. I have a feeling it's either dislocated or broken. I'm hoping for the former. Twisting slightly, I reach for my cell and see I have a fucking ton of missed calls, all from Ma. I also note that it's almost ten a.m. I've been unconscious for a long time. Shit.

I start the car, praying that I can drive. Right now, I need to get the hell out of here.

I call Ma's number and it connects to the car's Bluetooth. "Mallory," she cries. "Oh, Mallory, are you okay?"

"He found me again, Ma," I cry. "I'm going to get help. I need help, Ma."

"Baby," she breathes. "What do you want me to do? I'll come to you."

"No," I shout. "I need you and Shay to be safe. Please, Ma, please don't leave the house."

I hear her sobs. I hate that I'm hurting her. I wish there was something I could do, but everything is so fucked up right now. "Ma—"

"I feel useless. You're my daughter, Mallory. I should be able to protect you."

"You're protecting Shay, Ma. That's all I want. Please. I'll call you when I can. I love you. Please let Shay know that I love him."

There's a sharp intake of breath. "No," she shouts. "No, you will come home to him. Do you understand, Mallory? You are coming home to him."

I can't stop the tears from falling. I don't think I can. The pain I'm in is too much. I feel weak. I'm not sure I have the energy for this anymore.

"You do not give up," she sobs. "Please, love, don't give up. Your baby needs you."

"I love you," I cry. "I won't give up."

"I love you too, Mallory. Call me when you need me or when you're safe."

"I will," I promise her and end the call. I

know she hates that she can't be with me, but right now this is what has to happen. I'll never live with myself if something happens to Shay. I couldn't survive the guilt.

I grit my teeth, thankful Ma persuaded me to get an automatic car. I don't need to use my bad arm. I just need to get to Raptor. I know if I can make it to the clubhouse, I'll be fine.

I hope.

CHAPTER 15
RAPTOR

The clubhouse is abuzz with excitement. Today, Preacher and Ailbhe find out what the gender of their baby will be. I'm happy for my brother, but I can't lie, I'm fucking devastated that there's still no sign of Mallory. After speaking with Freddie last night, I thought she'd have been here. Fuck, I need to know if she's okay. She's been hiding for months, and I know it's because she's in trouble.

I'm giving her until Preach and Ailbhe's gender reveal thing is over and then I'm getting Freddie on it. He's here today, as is Maverick.

"Yo, Rap, any word on Mallory yet?" Shadow asks, his voice a little distorted from the laptop.

The brothers in New York are on a video call with us. They're waiting for the news just as those who are here are. Not to mention, the Gallaghers are here too. They seem to have adopted Ailbhe and her siblings.

"Not yet," I say through gritted teeth. I don't want to get into this shit now.

"They're here," Hustler says with a big grin. "Fifty on it bein' a boy," he says.

I shake my head. That kid doesn't stop trying to hustle. Everyone is used to his shit by now and no one will take him up on it.

The door opens and everyone goes quiet as we wait for Preach and Ailbhe to let us in on the news. "So?" Py asks as they take a seat, not letting them have a moment to collect themselves.

"It's a boy," Preacher announces, and the pride in his voice makes me smile. I'm happy for my brother. So fucking happy for him.

Cheers sound throughout the clubhouse and over the laptop. Everyone's celebrating and joyful. Preacher pulls Ailbhe onto his lap and kisses her. He's so fucking in love. The fucker almost lost it all, but he sorted his shit out and is three months sober now.

Freddie slides onto the seat beside me, his leather jacket creaking with each movement. "Still no word?" he asks, his voice filled with concern.

I shake my head, the knot in my stomach tightening. "Nothin'. You sure she was comin'?"

"Trust me," Freddie says, his gray eyes piercing into mine, "she's coming, and when she does, you've got a lot of shit to talk about."

Of that, I have no fucking doubt. My mind races with all the things I need to say to her.

"If she doesn't turn up, I want her address—" I begin, but my words are cut off by the sudden sound of the clubhouse doors crashing open.

"Fuck," I hear Maverick growl from across the room. My gaze snaps to the door, and my entire body freezes when I see Mallory stagger in. She's clutching her arm close to her body, her face a bloody mess, and there's so much blood covering her that I don't know where it's all coming from.

"Raptor," she croaks out, her voice barely above a whisper as she collapses to the floor. "Help."

My heart lurches as I rush toward her, my

boots pounding against the concrete floor. "Mallory?" I growl out her name as I kneel beside her. She's unmoving. She's fucking not moving.

Fuck. What the fuck happened? Who did this to her?

I scoop Mallory into my arms, her body limp and blood staining my cut as I carry her toward the nearest table. Everyone jumps into action. The women take the kids from the room, while my brothers rush outside to see if they can find out what the fuck happened.

Freddie is by my side in an instant, his jaw clenched tight as he surveys Mallory's injuries. "Fuck," he growls, his fists balling up in anger.

"Maverick O'Hara," Callie hisses at her brother. "You had better start talking. What the hell happened to that poor girl?"

The room is silent as I brush my hand over Mallory, checking for injuries. I feel helpless. I'm not a fucking doctor. How the fuck am I supposed to know what the hell is wrong?

"Everyone who isn't a patched member, out," Pyro shouts. This is now club business and anyone who isn't a fully patched member of the Fury Vipers isn't allowed to be here.

"Py, man," I say low. "She needs a doctor."

A heavy hand lands on my shoulder. "We've got one coming," Wrath assures me. "Bozo's friend is a doctor. She's going to help. Rest assured, brother, we're going to find out what the fuck is going on."

I turn and see Denis strolling into the room, his wife no longer here, nor is his daughter, Chloe. "Someone had better start talking," he says thickly. "Freddie and Maverick, the two of you know something, so fucking spill it."

Freddie runs a hand through his dark brown hair. "Last night, I met Mallory. It's been a while. She told us a lot of what went down and where she's been. Raptor, man, I know she wanted to be the one to tell you. But that's fucked now. About six months ago, Mallory was out one night. While she was out, her and a friend of hers were accosted by a fucking O'Leary—"

"She told me about that night," I say evenly. She even told me she was scared in case they found her. "Stephen killed the guy, right?"

Maverick's brows practically hit his hairline. "She told you what happened?"

"Of course she did. What has happened since?"

"Fuck," Freddie growls. "What she didn't tell

you, man, was that she was pregnant. She was around six months along that night. She gave birth three months ago. Congrats, man, you're a dad. You have a son."

The silence is deafening. "I'm sorry, what?" I say through clenched teeth.

"Not getting into the hows or whys about why she never told you. All I know is that she gave birth to your son, and it was when she was released from the hospital that she went into hiding. Didn't find out until last night what actually went down."

"Tell me," I snarl, beyond pissed right now.

"Mallory came home with Shay. That night, Micah O'Leary broke into her house. He stood over her bed and threatened her at knife point. He blames her for the death of his brother. He stabbed her and sliced her open. I've only seen a little of the scar, but from what I've gathered it's a fucking lot worse than she's led me to believe. She's been scared, terrified, that he'll come for her." Freddie glances at her unconscious body on the table. "I guess that fear was right. We shouldn't have fucking let her go home alone."

Maverick nods. "Shit, man, she dropped both Freddie and I home. We thought she was safe.

Had we any idea what would happen, we'd never have left her."

"Where's my son?" I ask, still fucking unable to wrap my head around that shit. Right now, I just need the doctor to come and sort Mallory out and to locate our son.

"We don't know," Maverick replies. "She hasn't given anyone the address. But he's with Mallory's mam, Jayne."

"Smart," Pyro says. "Fuck, where's her cell? Surely she'll have her mom's number saved?"

"Prez," Bozo calls out. "Gráinne's here."

A petite woman walks in, her blonde hair tied up into a messy bun at the top of her head. "What happened?" she asks, her voice filled with horror. "God, what happened to this woman?"

"Gra, we don't know. She's just shown up like this. We need you to help her. Can you do that?" Bozo says, his voice soft but firm.

"Of course, but Christ, Connor, this woman has been through hell." She doesn't hesitate to get to work, slicing through Mallory's dress. I bite back a curse as acid swirls through my stomach. From the base of her neck down to her breast and across to her arm has a jagged scar. It's pink and puffy, which means it wasn't done by a professional. Who the fuck patched her up?

"Shit, she's been stabbed. She's bleeding profusely. Christ," Gráinne cries. "I'm going to need a hand. This is going to hurt her. I don't have the painkillers to stop her from hurting."

"I've got you, doc," Maverick says as he steps forward. "What do you need?"

"I need you to keep her still. I need to clean the wound and then I'm going to have to stitch her up." Her gaze assesses Mallory's beaten body. "Someone has been working her over for a while now. She's got old bruises that are fading. Anyone know the last time she was beaten?"

I glance between Maverick and Freddie. Both of them are shaking their heads in the negative. When my gaze catches Denis', I see the anger and rage swirling in his eyes. Mallory is Chloe's friend. She's been a part of their lives for a while now. It's got to hurt seeing someone you care about like this.

Fuck, it does hurt, but she's kept so fucking much from me. She's kept my son from me. Why the fuck would she do that? I don't understand what possessed her to do that. It makes no fucking sense. We've got a lot to discuss when she's awake and up to it, but right now, the doc needs to focus on her. "Anyone have Jayne's number?"

"I have a cell phone here, in her pocket, if that's of any use?" the doc says as she pulls on gloves.

Maverick reaches into the pocket and hands it to Denis. "You'll be the best one to talk to Jayne."

Denis nods and walks out of the clubhouse.

"Brother," Py says low. "I get that you're angry and you have every right to be, but right now, she needs you to have a clear head."

I inhale through my nostrils, taking in deep breaths as I try to quell the rage that's swarming inside of me. "Why didn't she tell anyone?"

"Chloe and Jess have had enough violence in their lives. There's something you have to realize about Mallory. She protects those she cares about," Maverick begins. "When Chloe was being bullied in school, it was Mallory who beat the shit out of the girl who did it. She'll do whatever the hell it takes to ensure those she loves aren't hurt, and for Mallory, adding more violence to her girls was never going to happen, so she kept it to herself until she couldn't anymore."

Anguish fills Pyro's face, and I get it. His woman has had violence touch her, and he's grateful Mallory didn't bring hers to his door and trigger Chloe, but fuck, that's my woman and she's been through this shit alone. Christ.

"Jayne's on her way," Denis says as he re-enters the room. "She's been worried sick. She said Mallory never got home last night and she called her over a dozen times this morning when she woke and saw that she wasn't home. She finally got a hold of her and she said it was bad. She's been going out of her mind."

"She didn't look for her though, did she?" Preacher snaps.

"She wanted to go to her, but Mallory made her swear she wouldn't leave the house and that she'd stay with Shay. Mallory's worst fear is Micah getting her baby, and I'm not going to lie to you, Rap, those O'Leary fuckers are ruthless and they wouldn't hesitate in killing a three-month-old."

I bow my head. This is too fucking much. I can't fucking breathe. How the hell am I supposed to do this shit?

"It's gonna be alright, Rap," Wrath promises as he stands close to me.

I take everything in and realize every brother is standing close to me. I don't know if it's to offer support or to be on hand in case I need to be fucking locked down.

"Shit," Maverick says thickly. "Hey, Mal, you doing okay?"

"Shay," she whispers, her voice etched in pain.

"You're safe here, Mal. You're safe," he tells her.

She tries to get up. "Need to get to him, Mav. I need to get to Shay."

"I know, honey. I know you do. But right now, the doctor needs to patch you up. Your ma's on her way with Shay."

I've never seen anyone look so horrified in my life. I watch in absolute shock as Mallory knifes up into a sitting position and tries to push Maverick off her. "Get off me, Mav," she snarls. "Get the fuck off me."

"Hey," Freddie says as he starts to help. "You need to calm the fuck down."

She glares at him. "You need to fuck off," she spits. "Get off me. I need to go."

"You're not goin' anywhere," I say as I step forward.

The moment I speak, her shoulders droop and she glances at me. "I need to get to him."

I nod. "I know you do, but you're no good to anyone if you're dead. Let the doc patch you up, and then when she's done, he'll be here with your ma."

She begins to sob. "You don't understand. I think he's been following me. If he has, he'll know where we live. I told her not to leave. Please," she sobs.

"Fuck. Fuck," Freddie hisses. "Mallory, where will your ma be heading from? I can have some men meet her along the way, give her protection."

"Dalkey," she breathes. "Please?" she pleads.

My fucking heart is torn. I want to be so fucking angry at her, but seeing how distraught she is, I know I can't be. She's done everything she can to protect our son. But I'm still pissed she never told me about him. I'd have been here for her. Christ.

"We're on it," Tank says as he, Cowboy, and Freddie head out the door. "We'll bring your ma and boy home, Mallory."

My woman's eyes are closed as she sobs quietly. I can't hold back any longer. I push Maverick out of the way and stand at her head as she lies down. The doctor continues to do her job and clean Mallory's wound. "Tell us about Shay, darlin'."

"He looks so much like you," she says through gritted teeth. "He's such a smiler."

Pyro laughs. "Must get that from you then. Rap doesn't know what smilin' is."

Mallory's lips twitch. "He's perfect. Honestly, so perfect."

I close my eyes and savor her words. I have no fucking doubt that he's perfect. She's one of the sweetest people I know and I know she's a great mom.

"I called you," she whispers so only I can hear her. "The night I got home from the hospital, I called you. I had wanted to tell you in person, but when I gave birth, I called you."

"I didn't get a call," I say with a frown. What?

"I called your number almost every day since and it says it's disconnected or not in service. I know I should have told you when I first found out, and I'm sorry, but I really did try and call you once he was born."

I glance at Pyro and know that he's heard every word. "Brother, you changed your number when you got here. Your cell fell into the toilet and you had to get a new one."

"Fuck," I hiss. "Christ, I should have realized. Darlin', I'm so damn sorry."

She shakes her head. "It's okay."

"Mallory," the doc says softly. "I've cleaned your wound. I'm going to stitch you up now. It's going to hurt. I have some mild painkillers, but I'm afraid they won't be much help until afterward."

"It's okay, Gra. Do what you need to," Mallory slurs.

"You two know each other?" Pyro asks.

Maverick laughs. "It's Dublin. Everyone knows everyone," he quips. "But Gra works for Jer when needed, and with Mallory being practically family, she knows everyone who works for Jer."

"Unfortunately," Mallory sighs. "They're all cocky like Freddie."

"Sadly that's the truth," Graínne replies. "But I help out as I owe them, and without them I'd never have been able to get my medical license."

The doc begins to stitch Mallory's wound and I watch as my woman doesn't even flinch, not even a fucking whimper. It pisses me the fuck off. This is obviously not the first time this shit has happened.

"Okay, Mal," Gráinne says softly once she's finished. "How about I check your other injuries now? What happened to your face? Anything broken?"

"I'm grand," Mallory sighs. "Honestly, my face is the least of my worries. A washcloth will get rid of the blood. It's my arm I'm worried about. Fucker pulled it out of its socket."

Gráinne nods to Maverick and the two of them help Mallory sit up. She winces as she sits, and I'm wondering if she should be sitting up with her injury, but the doctor knows what she's doing. "Yeah, it's dislocated alright. Damn, he did a number on you, huh?"

"Tell me about it. But I'm alive and that's all that matters, right?" Mal says and I shake my head. The blasé way she's talking about what happened infuriates me. "We have an audience?" Mallory questions, her gaze on the laptop that's still on and has most of the brothers in New York watching.

"Those are our brothers, darlin'. They're in New York."

She nods in acknowledgement. "Okay, Gra, do what you need to do."

"You sure?" the doc asks. "I can go and get you some hardcore painkillers before I start?"

Mallory shakes her head. "No, just do it."

The doc's eyes soften. "Mallory, doing this without pain medication is going to hurt. You don't have to go through that pain."

"Gra, I need to have a clear head. Having painkillers is going to make me sleep and I just can't—" she pauses, her breathing hard. "I'm ready. Please, do what you need to do."

"Okay. I'm really sorry."

Mallory smiles at her before closing her eyes. I watch on, feeling helpless as the doctor gets into position. Mallory looks so fucking peaceful as she sits on the table waiting.

"Fuck," Pyro growls as the doctor reaches for Mallory's arm. "She's not goin' to pop that back into place without drugs, is she?"

"Yep," Maverick growls. "Fucking O'Leary. The sooner we find him and his father, the fucking better."

The doctor does indeed pop Mallory's

shoulder back into its socket, and once again Mallory doesn't make a sound as it happens.

"Damn. How the fuck did she manage that?" I hear Mayhem say from the laptop. "Balls of fuckin' steel."

"Okay, Mal, that's in place. I'm going to clean your face and then take a look to ensure you don't need more stitches," the doc tells her, and neither of them talk as she methodically cleans the blood from Mallory's face. She's got a lot of bruising, but thankfully, nothing looks broken.

"Hey," Callie says, walking into the room, her hands filled with clothes. "Chloe and I thought you'd want some fresh clothes."

Mallory glances at Callie. "Thanks, Callie."

"Oh, sweetie, are you okay?"

Mallory nods. "I'm grand," she replies, and I have a feeling she says that a lot actually. "Thanks for the clothes, Callie. I really appreciate it. I didn't even notice that everyone is seeing me in my bra and knickers." There's laughter in her voice, and while I love that she's making jokes, nothing about this situation is funny.

"Mo ghrá," Denis says as he walks toward Callie. The two of them begin to talk quietly.

"We good, Gra?" Mallory asks once the doctor finishes.

"Yeah. Just be careful of your arm and wound. Though judging by the scars and bruises you have, I don't need to tell you that."

"I'll be careful," Mallory promises her. "Thanks so much, Gráinne. I appreciate it."

The doc pulls Mallory in for a hug and holds her tight. "I'll be back in a few days to check in on you. If you need anything, call me, okay? Maverick and Connor both have my number if you need it."

Maverick helps the doc pack up her shit and I move back to Mallory. I can't hold back any longer. I pull her into my arms and she comes willingly, her body shuddering against me. "I've missed you," she whispers.

"Ah, darlin', I've missed you too."

She glances up at me. "Please don't hate me. I'm so sorry for not telling you about Shay."

"We'll talk about it later," I promise her. Right now, I don't want to have this discussion in front of everyone.

At the sound of car tires crunching against gravel, Mallory straightens, her gaze on the door.

Fuck, I'm about to meet my son.

CHAPTER 16
RAPTOR

Mallory's face is pale and she looks exhausted. Her body is tense and her gaze is focused solely on the door.

"Darlin'," I say softly. "You need to breathe."

She lets out a harsh breath and laughs. "I've been waiting for this day. I just didn't expected it to be this way. Me battered and with everyone watching."

"Why Shay?" I ask, wondering where the name came from.

She gives me that soft smile I love. "Your name's Shane. I wanted him to be a part of you too, even if I was a bitch and kept my pregnancy a secret. I didn't ever want you or him to think you're not important. I got scared and I fucked up. For what it's worth, I truly am sorry."

The sincerity in her voice is real. She knows she's fucked up and I'm glad she's taking accountability. I have so many questions, but right now, they're all on the back burner. I help her off the table and she grips a hold of my hand tightly. She sinks down onto a seat and I take the one to her left. Fuck, with all the shit that's gone down, I'm glad she's here. I could have fucking lost her. I'm numb. Angry but numb. I know once I get the full story from her, my anger is going to need to be unleashed, and I fucking pray that the cunt who harmed her is the recipient.

"Just to warn you, Ma's going to be really overprotective," she says, her voice louder than it had been.

"Can't blame her," Pyro says as he takes the seat to her right. "You were bleeding and beaten. How long ago did it happen?"

She glances at me before her gaze moves to her clasped hands. "Around one a.m. last night."

Acid burns in my gut. Christ. What the fuck?

"What happened?" Pyro asks, but before she's able to answer, the door opens and a woman with short black hair rushes into the building, a kid on her hip, her gaze moving around the room. Recognition hits her when she sees Maverick, but she doesn't speak. She continues to scan the room. I know the exact moment she finds Mallory. Her knees buckle, her eyes fill with tears, and she looks as though she's about to pass out.

"Fuck," Maverick hisses as he steps forward. "Jayne, she's okay. She's okay."

Jayne nods, pulling in a deep breath. "What did he do to her this time?" she asks, her voice filled with rage.

It pisses me off that it's happened more than once.

"Ma, I'm okay Gráinne patched me up," Mallory says as she rises to her feet.

"You need to sit your ass down," I snap. "You've just been fucking stitched up."

"Raptor," she sighs as she moves away from the seats and toward her mom. "I'm fine, trust me."

"Oh, that's Raptor?" Jayne asks with a raised brow.

I watch as Mallory's cheeks heat and she shakes her head. "Shut it, Ma," she hisses. "And give me my baby."

Jayne doesn't hesitate to hand over our son to her daughter. I keep my gaze on my woman, who snuggles our son close to her chest as she holds him tight. Jayne wraps her arms around the two of them, and I watch as both mother and daughter cry into each other's arms.

"Brother," Pyro says low. "This shit is beyond fucked up. The shit she's been through..." He shakes his head. "It's fucked up to admit this, but I'm glad she didn't tell Chloe. I don't think she'd have been able to deal with it."

I don't say anything. It is fucked up that he thinks that, but I get it. I don't agree with it but I get it. Chloe's been through something traumatic and is still living through the nightmares and aftermath. Mallory's been going through hell alone just to protect her friends. I fucking hate that she's not had anyone but her mom to lean on. I'm pissed that no one thought that something was going on and just let her slip into hiding without saying a fucking word.

"What are you going to do about the kid?" he questions.

"What'cha mean?" I ask, still not taking my

gaze off Mallory. She's talking in hushed tones with her mom, Maverick, and Freddie.

"You know what happened with Preacher," he says. "Are you goin' to ensure that it's—"

"Don't," I snarl, and it comes out as a deep rumble. My anger is now at the fucking surface. "You're my brother, my president, but don't fuckin' finish that sentence."

He raises his brows as he sits back in his seat. "I didn't mean—"

I don't let him finish. I'm not fucking doing this shit. "Just don't."

"It's okay," Mallory says softly. "We'll set up the test. Chloe told me about what happened. I never wanted you to think I trapped you."

I glare at Pyro. Fucking asshole. She heard what he said, and I won't have anyone make her feel like a fucking whore.

"Mallory," Bozo says as he joins us. "What do you mean Chloe told you?"

She turns to him, her eyes wide. "When I found out I was pregnant, I came to see Chloe, and she was talking with Hayley about how the women were trying to get pregnant at the club." She shrugs. "They were so angry. I get it; I would be too. I felt so bad for getting pregnant that I couldn't tell anyone."

Fucking Chloe. Damn it.

"Alright, we're done here," Maverick says, stepping in. "Mallory needs to rest and she and Raptor need to speak. So let them do that."

"I want to go home," she whispers and turns to me. "Can we do that? Shay has nothing here."

I don't hesitate. I get to my feet. "Your mom's driving, not you."

Her eyes soften and she looks at me like I'm fucking hung from the moon. "Thank you."

I walk over to her and take a look at the boy snuggled into her chest. He's so fucking gorgeous. Utter perfection, as she said he was. His eyes are open and they're staring at me. He's got his mom's eyes, so bright and beautiful. But he looks exactly like me. Fuck, it's like looking in the mirror.

"Shay honey, this is your daddy," Mallory whispers as she gently passes him to me.

I've held kids before because my brothers have children, but nothing could ever prepare you to hold your own child in your arms. Christ, it's like my entire world has shifted. He's everything I could have wanted and yet never knew I needed.

"Ma will drive us, if you want to be with him in the back?" Mallory whispers as she steps close to me.

I want that, but fuck, I need my own fucking ride. "Can his car seat be moved?" I question.

"The one in my car can be," she replies. "It's parked out front. Why?"

"I've got my truck. I'll drive us. It'll give us time to talk."

Jayne opens her mouth, no doubt to protest. She looks worried, and while I understand that she's Mallory's mom, I'm not going to let her get between us. There's so fucking much we have to say to one another. I'd prefer to do it when no one else is around.

"Jayne, no offense, but right now, I'm keeping Mallory and Shay close."

"Brother, I'll help you install it in your car," Wrath says as he strolls toward the door, a smirk etched on his face.

"Jayne, why don't you go see Mam?" Callie says softly. "She'll be delighted that she's not the only grandmother."

I watch as Jayne sighs and pulls Mallory into

her arms once again. The two of them seem close, a lot closer than what I recall Mallory had said previously. I'm grateful Jayne's been around to help her when I wasn't.

I keep Mallory and Shay close as we walk out of the clubhouse. Mallory's wincing with every step she takes, and I know she's in a lot of pain. I need to find out why she wouldn't take any pain pills when the doctor offered them to her. Wrath's already at my truck, the car seat in hand as he prepares to install it.

"I can do it," Mallory says as she steps forward.

"Darlin', the man's got two kids. He knows what he's doin'," I assure her.

She sighs. "Sorry," she says sheepishly. "I'm not used to the help."

It fucking burns me that she had no one other than her mom to help her. I don't understand why Maverick and Freddie didn't help. Fuck, even Stephen. That fucker set this shit in motion by killing that bastard. Why did no one check in with Mallory since that shit went down? I'll never wrap my head around the fact not one person seemed to give a fuck about her wellbeing.

"All set, brother. You good puttin' your boy in?" he asks, unable to keep the smile from his face. He's pleased as fuck for me, and I can't lie, it feels good to have my brother have my back. "He's the spittin' image of you, Rap."

Mallory laughs. "I do all the hard work and he comes out looking like his da," she says dramatically.

I glance down at my boy, who's watching me with those curious eyes of his. He's taking everything in and I fucking love it. "We're good, brother," I tell Wrath. "Thanks, man."

He slaps me on my shoulder. "Any time. Mallory, it was fuckin' great to see you again. Next time, stay a little longer. Hayley would love to catch up."

Mallory nods but there's no happiness in her eyes. Now I have even more questions to ask.

Once Wrath leaves, Mallory shows me how to put Shay into his car seat. She's patient as she explains it. "He'll be asleep before you even hit the city center," she says with a small smile. "He loves the car."

I help her into the passenger's side of the truck, and once she's secure, I hop into the driver's side while she inputs her address into the GPS system. "Okay, darlin', let's get this out of the way," I say as I start the truck.

"I was so scared when I found out I was pregnant," she says, hesitating to give me what I need. "I was around three months along when I found out. I wasn't sure how far along I was. I didn't know if it happened in New York or when you came here." She starts to wring her hands together nervously. "When I found out, I told Ma, and I wasn't sure what was going to happen."

I reach over and place my hand on her thigh. "Keep goin'," I encourage.

"I felt conflicted. I wanted to tell you but I had this dread. It felt so suffocating. I didn't want to upend your life. You lived in New York, Rap. You lived there with your brothers and you were happy. I didn't want you to resent me and Shay. I couldn't do that to our son. But I had so many doubts. I wasn't sure if I should tell you or not and it weighed heavily on my mind daily. I was selfish. I just didn't want to force you into doing something you never wanted to do."

"I get it," I say evenly. I'm still pissed, but I get her reasonings. She was eighteen, alone and pregnant. I lived over three thousand miles away. I get why she did it. It doesn't mean I agree with it, but I understand. "What about your conversation with Chloe?"

She glances out the window. "She told me about what was going on with the club women; how they were trying to get pregnant on purpose." There's a sadness in her tone and I fucking hate it.

"I'm goin' to make somethin' perfectly clear. I haven't fucked anyone since I met you, Mallory."

She turns to face me, her lips parted. I've shocked her. Good. "You haven't?"

I shake my head. "Babe, for fuck's sake. I gave you my name. No one, not even my brothers, have that. You think I'm givin' you that and goin' to fuck anything that walks? Seriously? I thought you knew this was more than just a casual hookup?"

She blinks, tears shining in her eyes. "What?" she breathes.

"Mallory, darlin', you really need to open your eyes and realize what's happenin'."

She inhales deeply. "I didn't know," she whispers. "I didn't know that was what you wanted. How was I to know? You're all I know, Raptor."

I grin, loving the reassurance she's given me—not that I needed it. She's not the type to sleep around, not to mention she was pregnant and had a fucking shit ton of drama going on. "Darlin', my name's Shane. Fuckin' use it."

Her lips twitch. "Really?" she asks. "After everything I've done?"

"You're the only one who gets to use it. What you did was fucked up, and I've missed a fuck of a lot, but I had some part in this too. I should have made it fuckin' clearer what was goin' on between us, not to mention given you my new number or a number for you to contact." I reach for her hand and intertwine my fingers with hers. "Now carry on. What else did Chloe say to you?"

"She said it was despicable for a woman to trap a man into getting pregnant. I panicked, Shane. I couldn't breathe. All I kept thinking was: is that what everyone's going to think about me? I panicked, and I'm so sorry. I really am."

"Alright, darlin'. You've explained why you kept your pregnancy a secret. I get your reasoning, though it doesn't mean I'm not angry. I've lost months with my son, with you. But I'm goin' to deal and we're goin' to move on."

She sobs softly as she nods. "Thank you. I always knew this day would come. I thought you'd hate me."

Christ, she really thinks badly about me. "That could never happen."

"When did you arrive in Dublin?" she asks once she's gotten her tears under control.

"I told you I was comin', didn't I?" I ask and she nods. "What I hadn't let you in on was that the club voted and now I'm the vice president of the Fury Vipers MC: Dublin chapter."

Silence spreads between us. "Wait... does that mean you live here now?"

I grin at the happiness in her voice. "Yeah, darlin', that's exactly what it means."

"Oh," she breathes. "But what about your family and the club in New York?"

"Darlin', I knew the moment I met you that you were somethin' special. Bein' apart was fuckin' torture. Pyro is my best friend and has been since he joined the club. He lives here and so do you. There was only one place I was comin'."

"Shane," she cries. "God, you gave up everything."

"Trust me, Mal, it's not everything. You and Shay are."

Her shoulders begin to shake as she sobs. "God, you're killing me. I don't deserve you, I really don't."

Her low self-esteem is something we're going to work on. I fucking hate how she puts herself down. That shit is stopping now.

"We're here," she tells me. "And I'm pretty sure Shay needs a nappy change."

I chuckle as the smell hits me. Damn, how can something so little make such a nasty smell?

"Let's get you inside," I say. Now that we have the secrecy about the pregnancy out of the way, we're going to unpack everything else.

No more fucking secrets.

CHAPTER 17
MALLORY

I've thought about this day for a long time and I always wondered what would happen. Shane has been beyond amazing. I thought he'd hate me, despise me for keeping his son from him. Instead, he's helped me and been so damn sweet. I don't know how the hell I got so lucky, but I'm so glad he gave me a chance to explain everything. I know my decision was selfish and I'll always regret it. I'm just very grateful that Shane hasn't pushed me aside. Instead, he's made it clear that he wants me, wants Shay. That's more than I could have ever thought possible.

"Where am I puttin' him, babe?" he asks as we walk into the house. Shay's babbling away to himself as he looks up at Shane. He's absolutely besotted with his da. I'm so happy they're together.

"I need to change him first," I say as I reach for the changing bag Ma left beside the door. No doubt she was in a rush when she left today when Denis called her. I know she was scared. She hates whenever I leave the house as she's scared what'll happen to me. We've been dealing with Micah's beatings together and she's seen what he's done to me each and every time he shows up. She's frightened that one day he'll kill me. We both are.

"You point me in the right direction and I'll do it. You need to rest," he tells me.

My heart warms at his words. God, I really did luck out with him.

I hand him the changing bag and tell him there's a changing table in the nursery. A place I haven't used much yet as I wasn't planning on moving him from my room until he was six months old. That's what my midwife told me was the best time, at least six months old. I love having him beside me and I feel a comfort knowing he's safe in his crib next to my bed.

While he's upstairs, I quickly make Shay a

bottle. He'll be hungry any minute. My boy's like clockwork.

I sink down on the sofa. I'm in so much pain, but I can't take any pain medication. I need to be alert in case Micah breaks in. He hasn't broken into our house since the night I came home from the hospital with Shay, but that doesn't mean he won't ever do that. I need to be level-headed and have a clear mind to ensure that if something happens, I'm ready for it. Beside my bed I have a baseball bat, not to mention a knife under my pillow. If he turns up, I'm ready to protect my mam and son with everything that I am.

I can hear Shane talking to Shay and it brings a smile to my face. Shay will grow up with his father at his side, and it's what should have been from the get-go.

"There's mommy," he says a while later as he comes to sit down beside me. "You doin' okay, babe?"

I nod. "Yeah, just tired." I hand him the bottle as Shay starts to fuss.

His gaze is unwavering as he studies me. "You not been sleepin'?" he asks and settles Shay into his arm to feed him. He's a natural. I know from what Chloe has told me that Shane's brothers have a slew of kids, and it's pretty clear he's a good uncle to them.

"Not really. I guess I'm used to it. When Micah does his shit, I tend to sleep for a bit. My body needs it. When that happens, Ma doesn't sleep."

"That shit's goin' to stop. You need sleep, Mallory."

"It's been hard," I whisper. "I'm terrified to sleep in case Micah breaks in. When he came that night Shay was home from the hospital, I was asleep, Shane. I didn't hear him come into the room. I woke up to him standing over me. He was so close to Shay. I was terrified. I thought he was going to kill us that night."

"What did he do to you?" he asks me.

I hate talking about it but I know he deserves the truth. I tell him everything that happened that night and since then. How he always finds me when I'm alone, whether I'm shopping or getting dinner. He'll always toy with me, hurt me, and leave me to pick up the broken pieces. I've had multiple broken bones from him. It's been hard to recover from what he's put me through. What he's put my family through. I'm not sure it's something we'll ever fully recover from. The first few months of your baby's life are meant to be precious. Shay's have been tainted with fear, pain, and brutality, thankfully not directed at him. I don't think I could live with myself if something happened to him.

"Darlin'," Shane says thickly. "Fuck, babe, how the fuck are you alive?"

I turn away as tears sting my eyes. I've been asking myself the same question for months. "He's not finished with me yet."

"He's not fuckin' gettin' you again. I promise you, Mallory, he's not goin' to fuckin' hurt you again."

His words are filled with determination and promise. I'm unable to hold back. I sob hard. I've always felt safe with Shane. Ever since the moment I saw him, I've felt so much protection and comfort. Having him here when things are the hardest they've ever been has given me so much comfort. I can't stop the tears that are falling. God, over the past three months all I have felt is pain and fear. Ma has tried her hardest to be my rock, and she has been, but having Shane here, it just makes me believe that this could all be finally over.

"I'm not leavin' your side. Not until that fuckin' bastard is found."

"You can't," I say. "You've got the club to think about."

He shakes his head. "You and Shay are my priority. If I'm needed, you'll both come to the clubhouse. It's safe there."

I tense. I'm not sure if I want to go back to the clubhouse. While Wrath was lovely, as well as Connor—someone I've known for a while—the rest of the brothers looked at me as though I was a bitch. I don't blame them, but I won't subject my son to be around that. "I'll get the paternity test done," I tell him. "I don't want there to be any questions."

"All anyone has to do is look at him, Mal," he says pointedly. "I know he's mine. I don't need a fuckin' test to tell me that."

"You don't," I tell him. "But there are always going to be people who wonder."

"Let them," he snarls. "Fuck them."

"Shane, these men are your brothers. You said it yourself that Pyro is your best friend."

He shakes his head, those dark eyes filling with rage. "It should never have been said."

"You can't blame them," I implore. "Especially after what happened with Preacher. They care about you and don't want to see you get hurt."

"By him questionin' Shay's paternity, they're insinuatin' that you're a fuckin' whore, and I'm not down with that. Brother or not, that shit ain't washin' with me." He's got so much anger in his voice. I hate that he's upset by the question. I'm not mad; hurt, yes, but I understand why there would be doubt.

"Please," I whisper. "Don't be angry about them caring for you. Let's just take the test and get it over and done with."

He shakes his head. "No. I don't need it done."

"I do," I tell him. "If we don't, I'm going to be judged even more than I already am. They think so little of me already that not getting it done will just make matters worse. Not to mention how it'll affect Shay growing up."

He's silent for a beat. "Fuck! Fine, we'll set it up, but this is for you and Shay. I don't give a fuck what anyone else thinks."

"You're amazing, you know that?" I ask, needing him to understand just how much I value him. He's one of the best men I know, probably the best. "Our son is lucky to have you as his da."

"Darlin', it's been too fuckin' long since I've fucked you. Our boy is wide awake and you're injured so I can't take you. Don't say shit like that or I'll forget that I'm a gentleman."

I laugh. "From what I remember, when it gets down to it, you're anything but."

Being around Shane is so fucking easy. I'm so comfortable around him that I don't need to worry about anything.

"The moment you're healed, darlin', I'm fuckin' you 'til you scream my name."

Shivers run through my body at his delicious threat. God, I can't wait for that day.

"Now, before you go and get any ideas, you need to sleep. I've got Shay. He's safe with me. You both are. I won't let anythin' happen to either of you."

A yawn escapes me, and I know he's right. I need to sleep but I'm not sure if I'll be able to. "Come on," he says. "Up to bed."

I do as he says, knowing that if I protest, it won't work. Once I'm lying in bed, I reach for my phone that's currently charging and quickly send a text to Ma, letting her know I'm safe and Shane's with me.

Ma: I'm with Nicola and Eric. They're letting me stay with them this evening. I'll be home tomorrow. I hope you and Raptor have managed to speak. I love you, Mallory. Be safe.

Me: Love you too, Ma. Have the best night. x

It doesn't take me long to drift off to sleep. I know Shay's safe. He's with his da. And I'm safe too. My family is alive and well, and that's all that matters.

CHAPTER 18
RAPTOR

I quietly lie Shay down in his crib. Mallory's fast asleep and hasn't moved since I walked into the room. She needs the rest as her body recuperates. I'm still fucking pissed about everything that went down today. She shouldn't have been touched, not fucking once. I'm going to find Micah O'Leary and I'm going to enjoy killing him. Hearing her recount what happened the night she returned home from the hospital after giving birth to our son was harrowing. I could hear the fear in her voice. It was like she was back to that time, reliving it all over again.

She's so fucking strong. Time and time again that cunt has hurt her and she's picked herself up and focused on our son. It doesn't matter that she's hidden away. I'm proud of her. She's done everything she can to ensure that our son is safe. There's nothing I could ever do to thank her for what she's done.

I press a kiss to her head and leave her room. I know she's checked in with her mom. Denis messaged me earlier to tell me that Callie's mom had let Callie know that Jayne's okay and she's spoken with Mallory.

I make it downstairs and reach for my cell. I've had multiple missed calls, the majority from Pyro. My brother fucked up and he damn well knows it. There's absolutely no justification for what he said today, especially with Mallory in the room. Just as I'm about to hit dial on Py's number to ream his ass out, I see headlights in the window. Someone's here.

I reach for my gun, something they don't use much here if at all. But with all the shit that's happened with Mallory, I'm not taking any chances. A gun is going to do a lot more fucking damage than a knife would. I open the door and see Maverick and Freddie walking toward me, both looking grim and pissed the fuck off.

"Sorry to disturb you, Rap, man, especially

with what today is for you, but we've got to talk. You got a minute?" Maverick asks, his gaze assessing everything around him.

Since I moved to Dublin, I've learned a lot about the hierarchy of the criminal world here. The Gallaghers are the most powerful family, but that's due to the size of them along with the way they have their organization spread out. It spans through Ireland, the UK, Spain, and the US. The Houlihan Gang has a lot of ties throughout Europe. They're next on the hierarchy, but since they work closely with the Gallaghers, they've grown in stature. Everyone is entwined in the businesses. Denis' wife, Callie, is the niece of the head of the Houlihan Gang. Jerry Houlihan loves his nieces and nephew, which is why Maverick is now his right-hand man. He'll be the one to take over the organization once Jerry steps down.

Not only is Callie Jerry's niece, Jessica is also, which means Mallory is close to Jerry through both of her girls. And that's what fucking angers me the most. She's tied to so many powerful people and yet not one person has been able to help her.

I open the door wider for them, letting them into the house. "Mallory and Shay are sleepin'."

Freddie nods. "Good. She looked dead on her feet earlier. How is she doing?"

I glare at him. "How the fuck do you think she's doing? She's in pain and terrified."

"We know you're pissed, Raptor, and we're going to make sure that Micah doesn't get away with this," Freddie says, raising his hands in surrender.

"Tell me somethin'," I growl low. "How long have you known Mallory?"

"Years," Maverick replies. "Since she was a kid. She and Jess have been best friends since they were in junior infants. They've been inseparable since then."

"So explain to me why no one, not one fuckin' person, knew that she was in hidin'? I mean, you saw that her house had been ransacked and that Mallory and her mom had left in a hurry, so tell me, Mav, why the fuck did no one try to find her to help her?"

"There's no excuse. We should have known."

"That fuckin' Maguire," I snarl. "He started this shit. Where the fuck is he?" He's not been mentioned at fucking all since we found Mallory.

"He's got shit goin' on right now," Freddie snaps. "His wife is also in hiding, something that

Mallory knows. Jess' father is a fucking cunt and has been severely torturing his daughter for years."

"He killed that fucker's brother, and now when that bastard comes to the surface and beats my woman almost to death, he's nowhere to be fuckin' seen. Tell me how that makes sense." My anger is at the forefront. I was never going to unload this on Mallory. She's been through too fucking much to have me spew shit at her. I need her safe and I need to ensure that I'm that safe space for her. There's no fucking way I'd jeopardize that by being a fucking ass to her.

"Like I said," Freddie says, "he's dealing with Jess right now. If you knew what she's been through you'd understand why he can't be here. But he knows what's going on and wants us to assure you that he's looking for Micah, along with Fintan—Micah's father. We're not going to let Mallory get hurt again."

My laughter is icy cold. "Excuse me if I don't believe that shit. I'll make sure my woman isn't found by that cunt again."

Maverick sighs. "I get it. If it were my woman, I'd be the exact same. We've all fucked up when it comes to both Mallory and Jess, but we're going to do everything in our power to ensure we rectify that shit and make sure neither of them are hurt again."

"Any idea where the cunt is hidin'?" I ask, needing to get a lead on the fucker so I can track him down.

"Nothing, but we've got all our men on it and I know Denis does too. With the Houlihan Gang, the Gallagher men, and the Vipers, it's going to be hard for him to stay hidden," Freddie tells me. "We'll find him, and when we do, he's going to be in for a painful death."

I know the smile on my face is anything but pleasant. I'm going to enjoy stripping strips off that cunt's skin. I'm going to take my time and be methodical as I kill him. He tortured Mallory; beat her over and over again. There's nothing about that fucker's death that will be easy. It's going to be painful, and I'm going to enjoy every fucking second of it.

"You've got our number. If there's anything you need, just call. If we hear anything about his whereabouts, we'll let you know," Maverick assures me. "We'll leave you be. I'm glad you're with her, man. She's one of the best and she has a deep capacity to love. Don't hurt her."

"I won't," I rumble, pissed that he thinks I'd ever do that. They don't know me.

He nods. "I'll see you around."

I wait for them both to get into the car before I close the door. That conversation didn't help ease my anger at fucking all. Fuck.

I sink down onto the sofa. I'm fucking tired, bone-ass tired. It's been a long-ass six months trying to find her, and now I have her back I can finally, fucking finally, have what I've wanted for a long time. My woman is under this roof. She and our son are safe, and that's what I'm taking solace in right now.

My cell rings, and I don't even have to look at the screen to know it's Pyro calling me.

"Finally," he growls. "Fuckin' finally. I've been tryin' to call you, brother."

"Been busy. What's up?" I ask. My tone isn't welcoming. In fact, it's clipped. He's pissed me the fuck off and he damn well knows he has.

"I ain't goin' to apologize for what I said, but I should have waited until we were alone."

I grit my teeth. Fucking A.

"How is she?" he asks. "She looked like she could pass out at any moment."

"She's asleep, as is Shay. She's in pain, but she's been so scared that fucking bastard will come back that she's not been sleeping. I'm not leavin', so I'm hopin' she'll sleep through the night."

"Wrath's none too pleased with us," he says. "He called me an ass and told me that Mallory's been a part of Chloe's life for years and we should have done more to find her."

"We all should have. It's just not us. The Gallaghers should have too. Everyone fucking failed her. It's fucked up that she's been through so much trauma and she's done it all by herself."

I hear his heavy sigh. "Why did she never reach out?"

I have a few ideas, and when she's feeling better I'll be delving into it and finding out what's going on. I know that when she was younger, her mom wasn't around much. She's not spoken about her dad, and when shit goes south, she's alone and has no one to help other than her mom.

"Any idea on where the fuck this asshole is?" he asks. "Denis has no idea. All he heard was that the O'Learys were up north in Belfast. Since Jarlath died, they've been in hiding. Fintan and Micah haven't been seen by anyone in months."

"Except Mallory," I snap. "She thinks that cunt is following her. I've got to say, with how good she was at hiding herself, he has to be keeping tabs on her."

"We need to have her vehicle and cell checked for trackers."

"Yeah, it's on my list to do."

"Brother, I know you're pissed, but we've got to sort this shit out," he says. I know he's right, but fuck... How can I let slide what the fuck happened?

"You fucked up, brother. You made my woman feel like a whore," I snap. "Tell me, if the tables were turned, what would you do?"

His silence is enough of an answer for me. "I'll apologize. Fuck, Chloe's goin' to kill me. She's already pissed that I kicked her out when Mallory was injured. When she finds out what I said, she'll go for my balls."

I can't bite my tongue any longer. "Mallory was the one who put a stop to Chloe bein' bullied. Mallory has put her friends above herself every fuckin' single time, and you practically call her a whore. Brother, you owe her more than an apology." I shove a hand through my hair. "She should never have felt alone. She should have been able to call any of us."

"I get it, brother," he says low. "We should have done better. We'll make it right. Whatever you need, we'll make it happen."

Fuck yeah we will. I'm not leaving Mallory alone. Fuck no. She's been through enough, and I'm not letting that cunt get to her again.

"I want that cunt found," I hiss. "I need my woman and kid safe, Py. I need them safe."

"We'll make sure they are," he promises me. "Anyone who tries to harm them will be taken out, brother. On that you have my word."

"Right, brother, I'm goin' to let you go talk to your woman and let her know that Mallory is okay. She's sleepin'. I'll have her call her in the mornin'." I end the call and take a deep breath. Fuck, today has been a fucking day.

I have my woman and my son, and right now that's all I'm focusing on. It's been a long time fucking coming, but tonight, I get to hold my woman in my arms.

CHAPTER 19
MALLORY

I blink awake as light shines into the room. I bite back the groan of pain as I try to move. My gaze moves to the crib beside me, and I see Shay fast asleep. His little sigh as he breathes is one of the cutest things ever.

I feel a heavy arm around my waist and the heat of Shane's breath on my neck. I had no idea he had climbed into bed beside me during the night. I want to sink back against him, but I don't want to wake him.

I stay stock still and continue to watch Shay sleep. This is something I tend to do a lot when I can't sleep. I love watching him. It's a comfort to me.

"Darlin', you doin' okay?" Shane says, his voice low. "You haven't taken any pain pills. You need any?"

I gingerly turn so that I'm facing him. He looks so handsome, his eyes filled with sleep. "I didn't mean to wake you."

"You didn't," he assures me. "You didn't answer. Do you need a pain pill?"

"No," I whisper. "I'm good. I'm still tender, but I'm not as sore as I was yesterday."

He slides his hand into my hair while looking into my eyes. It's intense but I love it. "You're so fucking beautiful," he says thickly.

I laugh softly. "Yeah, with the all the bruising I'm sure I look fabulous."

His hand tightens in my hair and he pulls me closer to him. "You're fucking beautiful," he growls. "You've always been beautiful."

"Shane," I whimper. He's killing me. He's actually killing me.

His gaze softens as he leans in to press a gentle kiss against my lips, the tenderness of the gesture contrasting with the raw desire burning in his eyes. I can feel his heart beating steadily against my chest as he holds me close. In that moment, surrounded by the warmth of our little family, I know we can overcome any obstacle together.

Breaking the kiss, Shane murmurs against my lips, "You're mine, Mallory. Never fuckin' doubt that."

Tears prick at the corners of my eyes at his words. I'm overwhelmed by the depth of emotion in his voice. "I want that," I whisper, my voice barely above a breath.

He brushes away a stray tear from my cheek and pulls me into his embrace, holding me as if he never wants to let go. "You know, I'm not lettin' you go, Mal. Bein' without you for over nine months was the worst nine months of my fuckin' life."

I close my eyes. God, he's the sweetest guy ever. You'd never imagine that with how he looks. He's over six foot, muscular, and has a few tattoos. He's got the death stare down to a T, but never with me. He's never been anything but utterly fucking amazing with me.

"I hated not talking to you," I confess. "Not texting you or calling you was the hardest thing ever, but I knew if I continued, I'd have told you about Shay and I didn't want to ruin your life."

He tilts my chin up gently, forcing me to meet his gaze. His eyes search mine, as if trying to figure me out. "Mal, baby, there's no fuckin' way you could ever ruin my life." His voice is filled with sincerity, his words wrapping around me like a comforting blanket. "I ain't goin' anywhere. You hear me? You and Shay are my fuckin' life."

I nod, feeling the weight of his promise settle deep within my soul. For so long, I carried the burden of my secret alone, afraid of the consequences it might bring. But I know now that I should have been upfront from the beginning. "Keep going, Shane, and you'll have me falling in love with you."

His smile lights up his rugged features. "That's good, darlin', 'cause it'll mean you're catchin' up."

My breath catches at his words. Holy shit. "Shane honey," I whisper, unable to even think clearly right now. I've always had a connection to Shane. There's always been more than just us hooking up. But I've never been in love. I've never felt that emotion before. But the more I'm with Shane, the more I'm coming to realize just how close to it I am.

His lips press against mine. He's so gentle. I know he's trying not to cause me any pain. Even though it's soft, it's toe-curling. I cling to him, a whimper escaping my lips as I press closer to him.

He pulls back, pressing a small kiss to my lips. "I wish we could explore, baby, but our son's probably going to wake up any moment and he'll be wantin' to be fed."

I smile. He's right, Shay's going to wake up any time now and he'll need his bottle. "I'll go make him one," I say as I go to get up.

"I'll do it. You stay in bed."

I grin. "You can change his nappy while I get his bottle ready, and if you want, you can feed him?" I ask, knowing that doing so is a great way to bond with him. My little boy likes to be cuddled and feeding is one of the best ways to snuggle with him.

The smile I get in return is huge. "That, darlin', sounds like a plan, but you're in pain and I don't want you hurtin' goin' down the stairs."

I press a kiss to his lips. "I'll be fine. Besides, I've got work to do and I'm going to do it downstairs while you feed him. Then we'll have breakfast?"

He deepens the kiss slightly, still being as gentle as he can. "Sounds good, but knowin' Pyro and Chloe, they'll want us at the clubhouse today."

I wince. God, I don't want that. Not only does Pyro think that I'd lie to Shane about Shay's paternity, but I'll have to deal with Chloe's anger and disappointment that I never confided in her about my pregnancy or what was going on with Micah, and that will lead to a whole new set of questions about Jess, and that's just things I won't answer.

"Alright, darlin', you go make our boy's bottle and then we'll talk."

I sigh. I should have known that would happen. But I trust Shane, and I feel as though I can tell him anything, including everything that has happened with Jess. I get to my feet and make my way downstairs. It's slow going, my wound pulling with each step I take, but it's manageable.

It doesn't take long for me to make Shay's bottle. Once it's done, I place it on the coffee table and reach for my laptop. There are a slew of messages waiting for me on the database for The

Agency, which means I have a lot of work to catch up on.

I get started as I hear Shane moving around upstairs in my bedroom. He's taken to being a dad a lot easier than I had expected, and I love that he's taking everything in his stride.

Shay's cries pierce the air, and within seconds I hear Shane's deep voice soothing him. I smile when I hear Shay's cries lessen. He's a natural at this.

Happiness is too tame of a word for what I'm feeling right now. I have everyone I care about in this house—Ma too when she comes home. I finally have what I've always dreamed of.

The sofa dips beside me and I turn to see Shane cradling Shay in his arms, gently rocking him back and forth.

"Hey there, little man," I coo, pressing a soft kiss to Shay's forehead. I reach for the bottle and hand it to Shane. Of course, Shay gets excited the moment he sees the bottle in his dad's hand.

I swallow hard when I see his tiny hand clutching on to Shane's finger as he guzzles down his bottle.

Shane looks over at me with a soft smile, his

eyes filled with unspoken understanding and affection. God, I'm so very lucky.

"Okay, darlin', tell me about your job," Shane says once he and Shay are in a rhythm. My little boy is happily drinking his bottle, content to be in his dad's arms.

"Have you heard of The Agency?" I ask him, wondering how much I'm going to have to explain.

His eyes narrow. "You mean *The Agency*, the one that's run by Melissa Harding Gallagher?" he questions, his voice hard.

"Yeah," I sigh. I guess I don't need to go into too much detail. "I email their clients with their next target."

He blinks. "Christ, Mallory," he hisses. "Are you fucking crazy?"

"I needed money," I snap. "Do you know how hard it was to watch Ma give up her dream job, the job she worked her ass off to get? She spent the past fifteen years making it up the ladder. She's now confined to working from home. She's not doing as much as she used to so she's lost a lot of benefits. Everything she worked hard for, Shane, is gone, and it's all my fault. I had to do what was needed to get money to keep a roof over our head and food on the table. I needed money to save in case we had to leave. Working for The Agency isn't something I wanted to do but it pays better than anything else and it means I can work from home."

The anger leaves his eyes and he glances down at our son. "Baby," he says quietly. "That call we had, the night Stephen killed that man. I remember every fuckin' word. You'd never seen anyone be killed before. It fuckin' affected you. How are you copin' doin' this?"

I close my eyes. "The nightmares are always going to be there, Shane. They're so fucking hard that I wake up in a blind panic. The second I wake up, I'm scrambling to find Shay. My nightmares aren't about Jarlath. Hell, they're not about the nameless targets I'm giving to the clients. I dream about Micah and the shit he's going to do to our son. I know he won't just stop with me. He's not going to let me off that easily. He's made that perfectly clear. I'm merely someone for him to toy with, and when he gets bored, he's going to hurt those I love." I swipe away at the tears that are falling thick and fast. "I can do this job because I've been through enough fucking pain that I'm numb to it all now.

I can do the job because it means giving me money so I can assure that our son is taken care of."

"Okay," he says with a nod. "I get it. If it's not affectin' you then, darlin', do whatever you need to do."

"Thanks for the permission," I respond a little tartly.

"Now, there's one last question and I'll leave you be for a while," he says, and I laugh. We both know that's bullshit. "Why are you worried about seeing Chloe?"

I sigh. "I guess I need to tell you about Jess," I say softly as I place my laptop down on the coffee table. I glance at Shay and see he's still content drinking his bottle, his tiny finger still curled around Shane's. "Jess' mam died when she was fourteen. It was unexpected and it changed Jess' life."

He nods. "I'd say losin' your parent at that age would do that."

"I got a call the night of her mam's funeral. She was in so much pain and needed help. I had no idea what happened to her. I met her close to my house, and she was practically doubled over in pain." I bring my legs up to my chest and rest my head against my knees. The memories of that night are still fresh. "I brought her home and Ma was gone. She was away for work. I think she was gone for a month that time."

He shakes his head, the disapproval clear in his eyes.

"The moment we got in the house, she lost it. She was screaming, crying, and she began to vomit. I had no idea what the hell was happening. I was so scared." I blow out a big breath. "Then she took off the big overcoat she was wearing. She was practically naked. God, Shane, it was fucking awful." I can't stop the tears from flowing as I remember what her back looked like. "Her dad had lost his mind. He was so angry that he poured lighter fluid on her back and set her alight."

"What the fuck?" he snarls. "You're not serious?"

I nod. "He hurt her so badly I didn't know what to do. I went to call an ambulance but she stopped me. She made me promise I wouldn't call anyone. She made me swear not to tell a soul. I was fourteen and stupid, so I made that fucking promise. I wish I hadn't. God, I wish I had called someone to help her."

"What happened, baby?"

"She wanted me to clean it up," I whisper. "I had no idea what the hell I was doing. We had to watch videos online to learn how to clean burns and to care for them. It was horrendous. She kept screaming and wouldn't stop. I didn't want to hurt her, but she wouldn't let me stop."

The sofa dips, and within seconds he's pulling me into his side, Shay still tucked gently in his arm. "Darlin'," he says thickly, his voice filled with emotion. "How the fuck did you manage to get through that?"

I lift my shoulders and shrug. "I don't know. I had to, I guess. Jess needed me. I cleaned her wound and helped her, but her dad came for her not even a week later and took her back with him. I knew he wouldn't stop. I couldn't ignore her. I had to push the anger, pain, and hatred I was feeling aside and make sure I was there for her."

"That's a fuckin' lot for a fourteen year old to take on."

"I had no other choice. She was alone, and she'd just lost her mam. I couldn't let her go through that alone."

"You're a good friend to your girls, Mal, but

why didn't you tell them when you needed help?"

"Jess knew about Shay. She was with me when I gave birth. She sent me a video of it. I have it saved to show you," I tell him with a smile. "But Jess and Chloe have both been through so much. I couldn't add my trauma onto them, especially when they're both still reeling from their own. I've watched as both of them have regressed into a nightmare. I didn't want to cause that again."

"Fuckin' martyr," he mutters, and I guess he's right. "You should have told someone. My brothers would have helped."

I swallow hard. "Even if it meant having Chloe break down?" I ask, knowing the answer to that question is no.

"They'd have called me," he tells me. "I would have been here."

I lean my head against his shoulder. "I know and I'm sorry. You're here now and I'm so fucking grateful. I'm tired of being scared. I'm so tired of it all."

He presses a kiss to my head. "You don't need to anymore, darlin'. I'm here and I'm not goin' anywhere. I've got you. I've got you both."

I close my eyes and savor his words. I believe him. I trust him with every fiber of my being. He'll do everything in his power to keep us safe, and if Micah somehow manages to get to me, I know Shay is safe with his dad. I'll be happy with the knowledge that my boy will have his father.

CHAPTER 20
RAPTOR

THREE WEEKS LATER

"You doin' okay, darlin'?" I ask Mallory. We're on our way to the clubhouse. It's the first day she's been back since she collapsed in it after being attacked. Over the past three weeks, I've spent every day and night at the house with her. Whenever I've had to leave, I've had Freddie, Maverick, or Denis stay with her. All three men have been continuously checking in on her and she feels safe around them. It's fucked up that my brothers haven't made her feel that way—except for

Wrath and Bozo—something I'm hoping will be rectified today.

"Yeah. I guess it's time to stop hiding."

I give her thigh a squeeze. "It's goin' to be okay," I assure her. "Once Chloe sees you're fine and meets Shay, she'll forget about everything else."

"Hopefully," she says with a shake of her head. "It'll be grand." She doesn't sound convinced. She reaches for her cell and sighs. "Ma's not replied to my texts since yesterday."

"Babe, you said it yourself earlier. She's probably at the spa with Nichola."

Her laughter is soft. "Yeah. I just wish she'd reply to me. I get worried about her."

"It's a normal response. With all the shit you've been through, it makes sense as to why you'd be worried."

We arrive at the clubhouse and I park out front. I spot Chloe waiting for us at the door. No doubt she's feeling the same as Mallory right now.

I open Mallory's door and help her out. She's still a little tender, but she's mainly healed from the majority of her injuries. Her arm still hurts and her wound is tender, but she's recovering.

"Mal," Chloe cries as she rushes toward us, wrapping her arms around Mallory. "God, I've been worried sick. I suck. I really, really suck at being a friend. I'm just glad you're okay."

I pull Shay out of his car seat and wrap my arm around Mallory once she and Chloe pull apart. "Let's get inside, darlin'."

The clubhouse feels like a haven compared to the chaos of the past few weeks. Mallory leans against me as we enter. It's a comforting feeling taking in all the familiar scents and sounds surrounding us. Chloe leads the way, glancing over her shoulder every few steps to make sure Mallory's still here.

There's so much guilt in her eyes, it makes me wonder just how much she's been told. I know Mallory would never want anyone to know the full truth of what's been going on.

As we step into the main room, the chatter dies down instantly. All eyes are on us, on Mallory, on Shay. I can practically feel the tension in the air, the unasked questions, along with the unspoken support. Wrath and Bozo stand up and greet us both with bright smiles.

I guide Mallory to a seat, Shay still cradled in my arms. He's just like his mom, taking everything in right now. Mallory's tense, no doubt remembering what happened the last time she was here.

Wrath and Bozo stand sentry close by. I'm not sure what they're expecting to pop off, but I'm grateful for their support. I catch Chloe giving them an appreciative nod before taking a seat opposite Mallory and I. It's not long before Pyro joins her, pulling her close to him.

"You're safe here, Mal," I murmur, pressing a kiss to her temple. She nods faintly, her grip on my hand tightening.

I glance around the room, meeting the gazes of my brothers. Each one them meet my gaze and then join us.

Chloe takes a deep breath, clearly steeling herself for what she's about to say. "I know there's a lot that I don't know, but I want you to understand that I love you, Mal. You're my best friend and I hate that you've been going through shit alone. You're never alone, understand? Never." Her voice is steady, unlike the emotions swirling in her eyes.

Mallory's shoulders relax marginally at Chloe's words, and a flicker of gratitude crosses her face. "I know. It's just hard to let people in. You, of all people, know that."

That was what Mallory and I discussed before coming here. Mal doesn't want Chloe to know the full extent of the pain she's been in, nor does she want her to know about Micah—something Pyro wasn't happy about but ultimately agreed to. We came up with what Mal should say, and telling Chloe she doesn't let people in was the best choice. While it's not the truth, it is something Mallory struggles with and something Chloe would believe.

Chloe reaches out, squeezing Mallory's hand gently. "I understand, Mal. And I respect your boundaries. Just know that I'm here for you, no matter what. We all are," she says, her gaze flicking toward Pyro and me.

Pyro nods in agreement, his expression serious yet supportive. "You're safe here, Mal. Both you and Shay."

My brothers nod in agreement and I feel a swell of pride for my brothers. The unwavering loyalty and love they have for me will never change, and that has now passed on to Mallory and Shay too. I'll be claiming Mallory as my old lady, and I can't fucking wait for that day to arrive.

Mallory manages a small smile, and it's a genuine one. She was worked up about coming here today, and in the end, it's been worth it. "Thank you," she whispers, her voice filled with emotion.

"Now it's time to meet my nephew," Chloe says, rising from her chair and reaching out to take Shay from my arms.

I hand my boy over to her and she presses a kiss to his cheek. I can't help but chuckle when he makes a kissing noise back to her. Chloe loves it and continues to kiss him, and he returns the favor. My gaze moves to Pyro, who's watching with a scowl.

"Brother, that's your nephew," I snarl. "Stop lookin' at him like he's the fuckin' devil."

Py's not in the least bit affected by my words. "The little shit knows what he's doin', flirtin' with my woman."

The clubhouse erupts in laughter and I sit back against my chair, watching how at ease my woman now feels here. I'm fucking glad. This is home, something that I want her to feel. I want my son to grow up around my brothers, around his cousins.

As the laughter dies down, Mallory leans into me, her hand seeking mine under the table. I entwine our fingers, feeling the warmth and comfort of her touch. I'm so fucking gone for this woman. I'm just waiting for her to catch up.

Chloe returns Shay to me, his chubby cheeks now flushed as he babbles away. He reaches for my finger and holds on tight. It's funny how someone so little can mean so much to you. The moment I found out about Shay I was in shock, but knowing that I had a son, I felt such a sense of duty, to love and protect him with everything I am. The past three weeks have given me an insight into how Mallory's been feeling, how protective she is. I get it. Boy, do I fucking get it. Every decision she's made since giving birth has been the right one, because it's kept our son safe. She tried to contact me after he was born, tried to speak with Chloe, but nothing worked. I don't blame her for that.

I have my family now. I have everything I could ever want right here in my arms. Mallory and Shay are my light. They're my world. They make sense of my life. I don't hold grudges against her for keeping the pregnancy from me. It's forgotten. It's forgiven. I'm here with them both now, and that's all I could ever wish for.

"Thank you, honey," Mallory whispers, her eyes shining bright with so much emotion.

We're at the clubhouse, in my room. Shay is with Hayley and Wrath as they've assured us they'll watch him tonight. They have their own son, James. I know they're wanting another child, but Hayley gave birth almost a year ago and is wanting to bond with James first before they add another kid to the mix. They already have Eva, who's nine and the image of her mother.

"For giving me everything," she continues, pressing a kiss to my lips.

I can't hold back. I slide my hand into her hair, dragging her close to me. It's been nine months since I've fucked her. She's healed and I need her. I slant my lips over hers and deepen the kiss, loving the soft moan she releases.

She's wearing my tee and nothing else. I slide my other hand along her thigh, getting closer and closer to her pussy. "Please," she mewls.

It's one thing I love about Mallory. She runs hot. So fucking hot. Sliding my tongue into her mouth as I push a finger into her pussy has her clinging to me like a vine. I've dreamed of this day for months. I've craved her for what seems a fucking lifetime.

Mallory gasps, her hips arching instinctively as I finger-fuck her. Her pussy clenches around my fingers and her breath hitches as I bring her higher and higher.

She pulls her mouth from mine, releasing a low groan. Her nails leave shallow marks on my back as I continue to pleasure her, her moans echoing in the room. Her body tenses and quivers with every thrust of my finger. I slip another finger inside, stretching her as I once again kiss her deeply, our tongues caressing one another.

"Please," she says hoarsely. "I need you."

I pull away, gazing hungrily into her eyes. "Are you ready for me, darlin'?" I whisper, my voice thick with desire. "You ready to take my cock?"

Mallory nods, her eyes sparkling with desire. "Yes. Give it to me, please, honey. I need you."

I position myself at her entrance. She's soaking wet, primed and ready for me. She's about to explode at any moment. Bracing myself above her, I thrust into her, feeling her tight heat squeezing my cock. She lets out a low moan, her hands gripping my shoulders. I begin to thrust, slowly at first, savoring the sensation of her body around me. She meets my thrusts, her hips rising to meet mine, her gaze never leaving mine.

I grit my teeth. The feeling of her tight, hot pussy is enough to send me over the edge, but I fight it, needing her to come, needing to feel her lose control.

I rotate my hips, pounding into her harder and faster. Her breath hitches, her eyes wide with pleasure and need. She's close, so close.

"Oh my god. Please, Shane," she cries out, her body arching off the bed.

Her pussy clenches around me, milking my cock for everything it's worth. It's intense, raw, and so fucking good. I can't hold back any longer. I thrust into her one last time, my cock jerking as I let go of the control I've been clinging to for so long.

I pull out of her and collapse onto the bed, both of us panting and sweaty, trying to catch our breaths. I pull her into my arms, needing to have her close to me. She rests her head on my chest.

Content. That's exactly how I feel. Content and in love. I never want this feeling to end, but the gnawing in my gut tells me something's coming. Something bad. I just pray we're ready for it.

CHAPTER 21
MALLORY

I sink down onto the sofa beside Shane and he pulls me in close to him. I go willingly, loving the comfort he gives me. "Your mom text you back yet, babe?"

I shake my head. "No. I don't know whether I should call her or not. I don't want to interrupt her time with Nichola, but I'm worried."

I'm probably overreacting and Ma's grand, no doubt sipping on cocktails with Nichola as they pamper themselves. Ma told me two days ago that she was going to a spa with Nichola and they were going for a few days. I was happy for her, so pleased that she was enjoying her time with her best friend, but not hearing from her panics me. It's probably stupid, but it's been months since I've been away from her for so long. Not to mention, with Micah out there I'm scared something bad will happen to her.

"If you're mom hasn't gotten back by morning, call Nichola," he says as he presses a kiss to my head. "Your mom will understand why you're worked up."

I smile. I love that he gets me. He understands what I'm feeling. He's without a doubt the sweetest guy ever. I've fallen so hard for him. There's no doubt in my mind that I'm in love with him. I'm just unsure how to express it.

"Do you miss New York?" I ask him as I snuggle even deeper into his warm body.

"Not really," he says, his hand splayed across my stomach. "Other than my brothers, I didn't have much there."

"What about family?" I ask. He's not spoken about them at all. I know nothing about them.

"Don't have any. My mom was a kid when she had me and did what she thought was right and gave me up for adoption. Problem was, the couple who had planned on adoptin' me found out they were pregnant when I was a few weeks old. By then my mom had upped and left."

"What happened?" I ask, horrified that

someone would give up a baby they were going to adopt. I could never do that.

"I bounced from foster home to foster home, for whatever reason. I wasn't adopted. By the time I was old enough to understand what was goin' on, I didn't give a fuck about that. I was immune to the bullshit of bouncin' from home to home. Once I aged out, I found the Vipers and joined the club."

"I'm sorry," I say softly. "It must have been tough growing up in different houses." I can't imagine how tough it was. I'd have hated it.

"It was what it was," he says thickly. "What about you? Your mom and dad, how was your relationship with them?"

"Dad wasn't around. I'm not sure why, but Ma told me recently that he was part of one of the crime families in Dublin and wasn't a great guy. From what Ma said, he was constantly cheating on her. The last she heard, he'd left town. I was about eight."

It doesn't hurt as much as I thought it would have. I guess the years of not having him around and finding out the truth about him has healed the pain of not having a family around.

"And your mom?"

"That's a different story," I sigh. "Ma tried her hardest to ensure I had everything. She worked her ass off to ensure that she was financially stable and could take care of me. But that meant she wasn't always around. I felt abandoned as I grew up. I was always left to myself. I could do whatever I wanted, whenever I wanted. She didn't seem to care. It hurt a lot. The neglect was emotional and it took its toll."

"It makes even more sense to me as to why you didn't tell me about Shay. You didn't want him to feel as you did."

I nod. "Yeah. I didn't want him to feel as though he was a burden, that you didn't want him. I think that would have broken my heart." I don't want Shay to feel anything I did growing up. It was heartbreaking and it affected me a lot. I'll never let Shay feel that way.

"But she changed?" he asks softly, his thumb caressing my stomach.

"Yeah. When I told her I was pregnant, we had a heart to heart. She had no idea that I felt so neglected. She hated that I was in pain and she didn't want me to feel that way anymore. She's been at my side since then."

"I'm glad she saw the light, darlin'. I'm glad

for you but also for our boy, who's got his grandmother."

"Shay's going to have a huge family and I love that, especially as neither of us had a family growing up."

"Fuckin' pleased our boy's goin' to have that."

My heart races as I look up at him, unable to resist his handsome face and strong body. "Shane," I whisper, my voice filled with love and gratitude. "Thank you for giving us a family. I love you more than words can express."

He pulls me onto his lap, his hands gently tangled in my hair as he leans in to kiss me, making my blood heat. Our lips meet and I sink into him. "I love you, darlin'. Never fuckin' doubt it," he growls.

His words are like a zap to my heart. I fucking adore that he didn't hesitate to tell me he loved me. His hands roam my body and it's like a switch has been hit. Our lips meet once again and I'm pulling at his zipper, needing him. "You want me, darlin'?" he questions with a smirk.

"Yes," I hiss as his hand tangles deeper into my hair. "Please, Shane," I whimper.

His grin is filled with wicked delight as he unzips his pants, exposing himself to me. I reach down and guide him, feeling the warmth and hardness of his cock. He groans softly in my ear as I position him at my entrance.

With a deep breath, I lower myself onto him, feeling him stretch me open and filling me completely. I gasp and my head falls back, my hands gripping his shoulders for support. God, I fucking love him being inside of me. There's nothing better than him stretching me.

Shane leans in, his mouth finding mine in a passionate kiss. "You feel so good, darlin'," he whispers, his breath hot and heavy on my skin. "I love you."

I smile into the kiss, feeling so much love it's hard to even think straight. I begin to move, up, down, and grind. Over and over again. I can't stop. It feels so fucking good. He's thrusting into me as I bounce on his cock. My pleasure is rising. I throw my head back, moaning as I do.

"Fuck yeah, darlin'," he growls as he grips my hips tightly and thrusts deep into me.

My nails claw at his shoulders as my pleasure hits me. "Oh, Shane," I whimper as my orgasm washes over me.

He groans low as he pistons into me, his cock thickening as he comes.

I'm breathing erratically, unable to pull in a deep breath. I collapse onto his chest, his cock still semi-hard inside of me. I'm so in love and overjoyed to be here with him and Shay. Once I know Ma's safe, I'll be so damn happy. I just need to make sure she's okay. I hate not hearing from her.

"Fuckin' love you, darlin'," he growls low in my ear.

My heart fills with warmth as I lift my head and look at him. "I love you too, honey."

Who'd have thought that we'd be here right now? Months ago, it didn't seem to be plausible. He was in New York and I was hiding from Micah. Now we're together, and it's as though we've never been apart.

I ROCK Shay in my arms as I try to settle him. Last night, he didn't have a good one. He was up most of the night crying. I think he could be teething. My poor baby is in pain and I hate it. Thankfully, right now, he's asleep in my arms.

"He doin' alright, darlin'?" Shane asks as he places a cup of tea on the coffee table.

"He's asleep," I say through a yawn. "I'm glad he is. I hate when he's hurting. It's awful. I feel useless."

He sinks down onto the sofa. "He's asleep, darlin'. Why don't you get some sleep now too?"

I shake my head as I gently pass Shay to him. "I'm going to call Nichola and see if Ma's with her."

He nods. "You do that. I've got Shay."

I reach for my tea and take a sip. My stomach is in knots as I dial Nichola's number.

"Hey Mallory, how's that sweet boy of yours?" she asks with a warm tone.

"Shay's okay. He's sleeping right now. I think he's teething," I reply, exhaustion evident in my voice. God, I'm bone tired. Shane's right, I should probably be sleeping while Shay's sleeping.

"Aw, poor boy. Teething is the worst. Is everything okay?" she asks with genuine concern.

"Just wondering if Ma's there. I haven't spoken to her in a few days," I say hesitantly.

Silence spreads through the line and I can feel my anxiety rising. "Mal, sweetie, I haven't seen your mam in a couple of days. She left three days ago, saying she wanted to go home and be with you. It didn't surprise me, seeing as you two are so close. She also mentioned wanting to set up a spa date with me," Nichola explains.

My stomach drops and my heart shatters at her words. "I haven't seen her," I say, trying to remain calm but feeling a sense of panic creeping in. My mind races with thoughts of where my mam could be. One name just keeps popping into my head. Micah.

"I'll call Jerry. Sweetie, we'll find her," she promises me. "Don't borrow trouble, Mal. I'm sure there's a perfectly good explanation."

"Okay," I breathe, my gaze meeting Shane's. His brows knit together as he watches me, his face filled with concern. "Let me know if you hear anything."

"I will," she promises me. "You do the same, please."

We end the call and I stare at Shane, gripping hold of my cell as I do. My heart is racing as a knot forms in the pit of my stomach.

"Talk to me, darlin'," Shane says, his voice low. "Baby, what the fuck's happened?"

I swallow hard. "Nichola hasn't seen Ma in three days, Shane. Three fucking days."

His eyes darken and he glances down at Shay before turning back to me. "We're goin' to find her."

I gasp, my heart breaking. "He has her, doesn't he?"

"No, baby," he says thickly. "We don't know that."

I don't respond. There's nothing to say. I can feel it in the pit of my gut. Micah has Ma. I should have called Nichola yesterday when I first grew worried.

I close my eyes. My mam... God, what is that animal doing to her?

CHAPTER 22
RAPTOR

THREE MONTHS LATER

It's been three months and there's no sign of Jayne. The woman has vanished. Mallory's devastated. As each day passes, she loses hope that we'll ever see her mom again. I can't lie; I'm relatively certain Micah has taken Jayne. It's fucked up. We should have found that motherfucker long before now. That cunt should be six feet under with his brother.

"You good?" Pyro questions.

We're on our way back from Belfast. We found Fintan O'Leary—Micah's father. The fucker's been holed up in Belfast, and no matter how many times we've beat the cunt, he hasn't given up his son's whereabouts. The fucker's not talking at fucking all.

We got a call from Maverick. Stephen's wife, Jess, has been kidnapped. Not only was she taken, but Callie, who was with her, has been too. Not only were we called in, but the New York Chapter was too, along with the Gallaghers and Gallos. Everyone is on the hunt for Jess' dad, Thomas. That fucker's finally getting his comeuppance and it's about damn time, but my mind isn't focused on Thomas and Jess. It's on Mallory, Shay, and finding Jayne. But with the club having such close ties to the Gallaghers, and with Jess being Mallory's best friend, this wasn't something I could walk away from.

"About as good as I can be," I say through clenched teeth.

"Mallory and Shay are safe," he assures me. "Both Tank and Bozo are with them. They're at home and secured."

"I know," I say, but it makes no difference to me. I want to be home with them. I want to be the one to keep them safe. But I'm needed to be with my brothers right now and that's all I should be focusing on.

"How is she?" Wrath asks.

We're in the truck. Fintan is tied up in the trunk and we're heading toward Maguire's farmhouse, where he takes care of business.

"She's tryin' to put on a brave face, but she's strugglin'. She keeps thinkin' about all the shit that cunt Micah has done to her, and she's thinkin' that's what he's doin' to Jayne."

"It's fucked up, brother," Wrath sighs. "But we're goin' to find them."

"You think she's still alive?" Py asks.

I can't fault him for asking the question. It's been on my mind for a while now. It's been three months. Three fucking months and nothing. Not a fucking clue as to where Jayne or Micah could be. Would he keep her alive this long? It would be better for her if he hadn't. That's a fucking long time to torture someone. But for the sake of my woman and our son, having Jayne alive is the only option for us. If Jayne doesn't make it, Mallory's going to be fucking devastated.

"I fuckin' hope she is."

"Same, brother," Py growls. "Here's fuckin'

hopin' that piece of shit in the trunk will give us the location to where his son and Jayne are."

The rest of the ride to the farmhouse is silent. I'm stuck in my fucking head about this shit. My woman is hurting and there's nothing I can fucking do about it.

I watch as Wrath and Preach get Fintan in position. They're not gentle about it. They're making sure they get their licks in as they strap him to a chair.

Pyro's cell rings. "Yeah?" he answers, his eyes hard. "You've found them?" he asks whoever's on the other line. "They hurt?"

Fuck, I sure as fuck hope not. If Jess is hurt, Mallory's going to lose her shit. She still feels a lot of fucking guilt for not opening up about what the hell went down with Jess when they were teens. She was fourteen, for fuck's sake. She was alone and had no one to talk to. She did what she thought was best for her and her friend, and knowing what that fucker Thomas did, I know he'd have hurt Mallory if she had told anyone about what was going on.

"We're on our way. Are Jess and Callie okay?" Pyro questions. "Fuck. Alright, we'll be there as soon as we can."

Almost as one, we move back to the truck. "That was Maverick. They finally have their location. No one has any idea if the women are hurt, but they've had confirmation that Thomas and the women are there."

I roll my shoulders, glad this fucking thing is almost over. Once we deal with Fintan and Thomas, we'll find Micah. We'll find out where that cunt is and then I'm going to kill him. I'm going to take my time and methodically kill him.

We arrive at an old as fuck cemetery. Everyone is here, waiting, their faces hard and filled with anger. We exit the truck and I move toward Ace, who's waiting with the rest of my New York brothers. Fuck, it's good to have them here. It's been a while. I'm hoping they'll stay and help me find Jayne and Micah.

"How you doin', brother?" Ace questions. "You good?"

"I'll be better once all this shit is over with."

He nods. "I get that. Gotta tell you, the women are here and they're dyin' to meet your son and woman."

I grin. Despite the shit storm we're in, I fucking grin. "She'd love that."

My woman loves that our son is surrounded

by family, that he's got a lot of people who'll love him. Mallory wants Shay to have a huge family, something that neither of us had.

"Stephen," Danny, Denis' eldest son, says, moving toward Stephen. "Look, man—"

"What's he done to her?" Stephen growls. "Tell me what the fuck is going on."

"She's tied to a table. I could only see that. Da told me to wait back for you to get here."

Stephen nods, his jaw clenched. "Denis," he calls out, his voice thick and filled with emotion.

I'd be the fucking same if the tables were turned. Jess is his wife. I'd be losing my shit right now if it were Mal in Jess' place.

"Here," Denis replies, stepping forward. "From what Danny says, Callie isn't injured. Just tied up."

"But you'll check that yourself," Stephen replies, his gaze firmly on the mausoleum his wife is currently tied up in.

"I'll be with you," Mav says, placing his hand on Stephen's shoulder. "Denis has Callie and we'll make sure Thomas doesn't get away."

"I'll need you to take him down, Mav," Stephen grunts, his lips pulled into a snarl.

It doesn't take us long to surround the mausoleum. We wait, watching as they enter the building. It's like waiting for an eternity, but when they exit the building, I see Denis holding his wife. She's got tears streaming down her face, but other than that, she seems as though she's uninjured. Stephen emerges next and he's holding Jess in his arms, a jacket wrapped around her. She's unconscious. Seeing her like that reminds me of Mallory when she crashed into the clubhouse.

I need to be with my woman. I can't fucking deal with standing around and waiting for shit to happen. I know my brothers have this shit in hand. "I'm headin' home," I tell Pyro once everyone begins to disperse, most of them heading toward the hospital to check in on Jess and Callie.

Pyro nods. "Go. We'll let you know if we have a location on Micah. Go be with your family, brother."

I don't wait around. I jump into my truck knowing my brothers will be using the van to escort Thomas to Stephen's farmhouse. I drive like a crazy fucker to get to the house, needing to make sure my family is safe.

Mallory crashes into me the moment I step into the house. I lift her into my arms and she wraps her legs around my waist. Fuck, having her in my arms is the best feeling in the fucking world. "You're home," she breathes. "Is Jess okay?"

"She's on her way to the hospital, darlin'," I say low, hating that I'm the one who's breaking this shit to her. "Got a call from Maverick when I was on the way home to you. That cunt burned her again."

She begins to sob in my arms, her body trembling against me. I fucking hate that she's hurting but she needs to know. "Is she okay?" she asks through her tears.

"She's in surgery. It's goin' to take some time, but when she's out, Maverick will call and let us know how she is."

I keep her in my arms as she tries to calm down. I turn to Bozo and Tank. "Thanks for stayin' here," I say, giving them a chin lift. "I appreciate you bein' here."

They rise to their feet, both grinning like loons. "Your woman can cook, brother. You need to bring her to the clubhouse. Her cooking's the bomb," Tank says while smirking. "No thanks needed, especially when your woman cooks."

Mallory shakes, and this time it's not from crying but from laughter. "Those guys are hilarious—"

A pain-filled cry rents the air. Everyone freezes at the sound. I drop Mallory to her feet and start barking orders. "Darlin', go upstairs to our boy and stay there. Tank, you go out back. Bozo, you're with me. No one gets into this house."

The wail ends just as abruptly as it began, and it makes the hairs on the back of my neck stand on end.

Everyone moves, Mallory taking the stairs two at a time as she races to our son. Tank moves with purpose to the back of the house, his fingers clenched around the butt of his gun that's at his back. Bozo and I exit the front door, our guns raised as we scope the area.

We scan our surroundings thoroughly. Wherever the sound came from, it's gone now. There's no sign of anyone being out here. But that noise wasn't imaginary. Someone was fucking screaming. Could it have been a ploy to get us away from the house? There's no way for them to get past any of us. We'd have seen them if they even tried to get past us.

"Fuck," Bozo grunts. "The fuck was that?"

I shake my head. "I don't fuckin' know." I head back to the house. "You two can head on back to the clubhouse," I tell the guys once we're in the kitchen.

"I'm stayin' here," Bozo tells me. "That was fucked up shit and I ain't leavin'."

Tank grins. "Your woman goin' to cook breakfast?"

I laugh. "Sure, why not. I'm goin' to make sure Mallory's good. You two make yourselves at home."

"You're okay," Mallory breathes as I enter the bedroom. She's sitting on the bed, a knife in her hand. She's ready for anything or anyone who comes through the door.

"It's all good, darlin'. You can put the knife down."

The relief that shines in her eyes makes my heart clench. Fuck, she's terrified. "It's all goin' to be okay," I promise her. "Tank and Bozo are spendin' the night. You and Shay are safe. Get into bed, darlin'. We're goin' to get some sleep."

She gives me a soft smile and I know that she's okay, but this shit is coming to an end. I can fucking feel it.

CHAPTER 23
MALLORY

I come awake as he pushes his finger inside of my sleek, wet heat. I'm unable to hold back a groan. "Shane," I whimper as I grind down against his finger.

His breath is hot against my neck. "Fuck, darlin'," he growls, pressing a kiss to my throat. "I've never been harder than I am right now. I'm about ready to burst. I'm going to fuck you, and once all this shit is over, I'm claimin' you as my old lady."

I whine, still grinding against his finger. "Yes," I hiss, his fingers stretching me.

He finger-fucks me hard, bringing me to the edge. Just as I start to build, he withdraws from me. "Asshole," I growl. I was so damn close.

He chuckles and spins me around so we're facing one another. "Gonna fuck you now, darlin'." He growls as he pushes me onto my back, his cock lined up to my entrance and he plunges deep inside of me. "You goin' to be my good girl and keep quiet?"

"Yes," I cry out as he continues to drive deep inside of me.

His eyes flash with heat. "Good," he growls, tilting my hips and plunging inside of me again.

I can't hold back as my orgasm tumbles over me. My nails rake down his chest. He hisses out a breath as I dig deep into his flesh. "Fuck," he grunts. The final thread of his control breaks and he fucks me without a care.

"More," I whine, needing more. There's no finesse anymore. We're both trying to reach our peak. I love having him inside of me. There's no one else for me but Shane. He's my everything.

He thrusts deep, twisting his hips and pounding into me.

Reaching up, I wind my arms around his neck and fuck him back, needing to come again. I'm on the cusp, ready to explode at any moment. He's driving deep inside of me, his cock stretching me with every thrust, and the burn only adds to the pleasure.

He snarls, his lips crashing down against mine, and that's all it takes for me to detonate. My cries are swallowed by his mouth.

His cock swells inside of me as he drives into me once—twice—thrice, before he stills, coming hard as he pulls back from me and releases a long, low groan.

"Now that's a way to wake up," I breathe, glancing at the crib and realizing Shay is no longer there.

"Calm, baby. He's with Bozo and Tank. He woke and I changed his diaper and fed him. He's happy bein' with my brothers."

I slap his chest. "You just wanted to have your wicked way with me, didn't you?"

His chuckle is deep, and as his cock is still inside of me, I can't help but moan as it slides deep into me. "Shane," I whine, pressing a kiss against his lips.

"Alright, baby, let's shower and then we'll get you somethin' to eat."

I grin at him. "Sounds like heaven."

He grips my hips and holds me close to him as he gets off the bed. I wrap my legs around his waist and hold on for dear life, but I should know that he'd never drop me. He walks us to the bathroom, his fingers kneading my ass cheeks the entire way.

"Love you," I say with a grin as I look up at him. It never fails to amaze me just how handsome and sexy he really is.

He glances down at me, his eyes filled with heat and lust. He's just had me and I can feel his cock thickening inside of me. "Love is too tame a word for what I feel for you, darlin'. Too fuckin' tame."

I pull in a sharp breath. Holy shit, he is the sweetest guy ever.

"Gonna fuck you again now, darlin'," he says thickly as he turns on the shower.

I grin. "You're insatiable, honey."

He grips my ass and thrusts deep inside of me. I groan, throwing my head backward. "Only for you," he growls.

"Please, honey," I beg. "I need you."

"I know what you need, darlin'," he says, his lips going to my neck, where he sucks on my skin, his fingers digging harder into my ass as he thrusts harder and deeper than before.

"God," I moan, my fingers diving into his

hair. I'm unable to keep my volume down. I cry out as he continues to pound into me.

His teeth nip at my neck and it sends me spiraling. I tug on his hair as my orgasm washes over me. "Love you," I cry out as I come.

He grits his teeth as he fucks me into oblivion. I'm crying out with every thrust. Unable to hold back, he pushes inside of me once more and warm cum fills me as he explodes. "Love you too," he pants, resting his forehead against mine.

I'm so fucking in love. I just wish Ma was here to see how happy Shay and I are with Shane. I fucking miss her. I miss her so damn much. I just want to know where she is and that she's okay.

"Morning," I greet Tank and Bozo as I enter the kitchen. Shane's already seated and has Shay on his lap.

"'Tis a fabulous mornin', wouldn't you say, Mallory?" Tank goads me. I feel my cheeks burning with heat. I'm not going to let him embarrass me.

"Jealous, Tank?" I ask with a raised brow, making both Bozo and Shane laugh.

"Fuck yeah," he says. "My guy got it twice this mornin'. Anyone would be jealous."

Shane slaps the back of his head. "Shut it, dick."

I giggle as I begin to make breakfast. A full Irish breakfast is the best way to start the morning, and I owe Tank and Bozo for staying the night and taking care of me and Shay. I'm smiling as I cook while listening to the guys laugh and joke around.

Once I have the breakfast dished out, I take Shay from Shane's arms and let him have his breakfast in peace. I take Shay upstairs to change his nappy. I begin to tickle his belly once I have him down on the changing table. His laughter fills the air as he giggles. It's music to my ears listening to his laughter. It's a sound I could bottle up and keep for the rest of my life.

Once I've finished and he's all clean and changed, I bring the nappy downstairs. The guys are still talking. Their deep voices feel soothing to me, and I'm settled. Even though Ma's not here, I'm safe with Shane and the guys.

"Who's a good boy?" I say to Shay as we head

outside to take the nappy to the trash bin. I run my nose along his cheek and listen to his giggle. I repeat it over and over again as I walk toward the trash.

"There we go, all clean," I say with a grin as he makes a claw to grab my nose. I shake my head, and something across the street catches my eye.

My body turns, and in an instant, it freezes. My eyes focus on the figure hanging from the top window of the neighboring building. A lump forms in my throat as I recognize who it is. My knees give out and I collapse to the ground, a piercing scream escaping my lips. Everything around me seems to be moving in slow motion.

"Mallory?" a voice calls out behind me.

I feel strong hands grip me, pulling Shay from my arms, and then seconds later I'm being lifted into the air and pressed against a solid chest. "Fuck, darlin'." Shane's deep voice rumbles in my ear. "I'm so sorry, baby."

But his embrace offers no solace amidst the chaos. The smell of his cologne mixes with the stench of death and overwhelms my senses. Tears cloud my vision as I struggle to process what has happened.

My mam... God, my mam. She's hanging from the window across the street. Her once vibrant eyes are now wide and lifeless. It's an image that will haunt me forever.

A suffocating emptiness swallows me whole as I'm crushed against Shane's chest, unable to tear my gaze away from her still form.

Shane's grip tightens around me, a silent anchor in the storm raging inside me. The world blurs around the edges as I cling to him, trying to find some sense of stability amidst the overwhelming grief.

Images of her laughing hit me like a freight train. I remember her touch, and the feel of her unwavering love, each memory like a knife twisting in my already shattered heart.

I let out a guttural sob, the pain of it reverberating through my entire being. I stare at the lifeless figure hanging in the window across from me, and I know nothing will ever be the same again. The world I once knew has been irrevocably altered. Shay's not going to know how amazing his grandmother was.

Thinking about Ma, something else hits me. I push myself away from Shane's grasp, my eyes filled with tears. I clench my jaw so as not to sob right now.

Shane's expression is pained, his own grief mirroring mine. He feels deeply for me, for our son. "Darlin', don't—"

"He could be there," I say through gritted teeth, trying to pull from his arms. "He could still be in the house."

"Trust me, darlin'; Tank's called the brothers. They're on the way. It's goin' to be okay."

Tears stream down my face as I shake my head in disbelief. "How?" I sob, my voice breaking. "How is it going to be? She's gone, Shane. She's gone." My heart aches with each word.

My breathing becomes choppy as I gasp for air. "That cry," I gasp, gripping my hair in frustration. "That cry last night. It was her, wasn't it?" The image of her distraught face flashes before me once again and I crumble to the floor. The painful cry we heard last night will be etched into my mind forever.

Oh God, she was alive last night and now she's gone.

"Fuck," Shane growls as he scoops me into his arms and holds me close. I sob against his chest, my entire body trembling.

I can't stop the tears. It's too much. It's too fucking much. I close my eyes and sink deeper into Shane's embrace. He walks us into the house and lies me down on the bed. He holds me tight and I cling to him like he's my lifeline. It's not long until I cry myself to sleep.

I wake up to hushed tones and open my eyes. They feel so heavy, just as my body does. Shay is fast asleep beside me. I watch as his chest rises and falls. I'm numb right now. I have no idea what to feel. I'm just in such an empty space.

"It's fucked up, brother," I hear Pyro say. "That cunt has been livin' across the road to Mallory for God knows how long."

I freeze, unable to believe what I'm hearing.

"Fucker's been watchin' her," Shane snarls. "Just as she thought he was."

"You think he had Jayne there the whole time?" Pyro questions, and my tears once again start to fall.

We could have helped her. God, we could have saved her.

"I want Mallory and Shay at the clubhouse," Shane says, his words filled with anger. "That fucker could get her," he snarls. "I can't have that. I can't lose either of them."

I reach for Shay's hand and he clenches it around my finger. Shane's right, we can't be here. We're not safe.

It's all too much. There are too many memories of Ma.

God, I miss her so fucking much.

What the hell am I going to do without her?

CHAPTER 24
RAPTOR

It's been two weeks since Mallory found her mom's dead body hanging from the neighboring window. She's become withdrawn and sullen. She's fucking broken. I wish I could help her, but there's nothing anyone can say to make her feel better. She's lost her mom.

"Darlin', you good?" I shout up the stairs.

She's getting herself and Shay ready. Today, he's got his six-month check-up at the doctors, and while he has to go, I know the dangers of letting Mallory and Shay go alone. Over the past two weeks, neither have been left alone by themselves. They're always with me or my brothers.

Today, I've ensured that when we go to the doctor's office, we're covered. Wrath, Bozo, and

Cowboy are coming with us. I'm not taking any fucking chances. None at fucking all.

"We're ready," she shouts as she walks down the stairs. She's got Shay sitting on her hip. My boy's dressed in a Harley Davidson tee and jeans. He looks so fucking cute. "We're running late. I'm sorry."

I pull her into my arms. "Chill, darlin', yeah?" I say, knowing how stressed she's going to get if she thinks about being late. "We're leavin' now. We'll be there in plenty of time."

She releases a deep breath. "Okay, let's go."

I take a hold of her hand and we walk out of the clubhouse. My brothers are already positioned at the doctor's office. I want them scoping out the place ahead of our arrival.

"How you feelin', darlin'?" I ask once we're in my truck.

"Tired," she sighs. "But I'm okay. Taking it day by day."

I reach across and splay my hand on her thigh. "I'm here if you need to talk."

Over the past two weeks, she's not spoken about her mom at all. She's bottling everything up and keeping it to herself. During the funeral, she sat there stoic. She didn't cry. She just looked ahead as the funeral service went ahead. Chloe has tried to help her, but she's brushing everyone off and acting as though she can get through it all herself.

"I'm scared," she confesses. "I'm so terrified that he's going to find us and he's going to hurt Shay. I've lost Ma, Shane. I can't lose anyone else."

I tighten my grip on the steering wheel, feeling the weight of Mallory's words heavy in the air between us. The fear that clenches at her voice rattles me to the core. Having Micah out there, his whereabouts unknown, it means he could strike at any moment.

"We won't let anything happen to Shay," I say firmly, trying to reassure her as much as possible. "I promise you, darlin', we'll protect him with everything we've got. We'll protect you both."

She nods slowly, the fear still flickering in her eyes. "I know you will, Shane. I trust you."

As we pull up to the doctor's office, Wrath, Bozo, and Cowboy situate themselves around us, their presence hidden from Mallory. I know if she saw them, she'd freak the fuck out.

I sit in my truck as she walks into the office,

clutching Shay tightly as she makes her way inside.

I drum my fingers on the steering wheel, my gaze scanning the parking lot. I'm on edge. I fucking hate this shit; being constantly on the look-out, wondering when that cunt's going to turn up.

I see Bozo moving toward me. I slide out of the truck and meet him halfway. "What's up?"

"He's here," he snarls. "The black Ford Mondeo in the corner."

The vehicle pulled in less than a minute ago. I watched as the car entered the lot and parked. "You positive?"

He nods. "Oh yeah, it's him."

My grin is sinister. We finally have him. Fucking finally.

"He does not get close to the door," I hiss, my blood running cold as I see the cunt exit his vehicle.

"Yo, Micah," Cowboy greets with a big fucking smile. "Long time no see, my man. How are things?"

"He's got this, Rap. Trust him," Bozo says low.

"Leighton, what's the story?" Micah asks, moving toward him.

I watch as Wrath moves around so that he's positioned at Micah's back.

"Nothin' much. Same old shit, different day. I had no idea you were back in Dublin. I thought you were up in Belfast?"

"I am, but I've got something to do. A score to settle, if you will."

Bozo and I edge closer. Cowboy's doing a great job of keeping that fucker occupied.

"Oh? Who's stupid enough to get on your bad side?" Cowboy questions, his tone one of ease, and he's got that big bright smile still on his face. He's keeping up the facade and Micah's falling for it.

"Some stupid bitch who fucked up. She's here today, and she has no idea that today's her unlucky day."

Cowboy's gaze slides toward me and I give him a nod, letting him know we're in position.

"That's where you fucked up, Micah," Cowboy says. The easiness slides from his voice and it takes a harder edge to it. "Mallory is family and you ain't goin' to fuckin' touch her."

Micah laughs. "Yeah? Who's going to stop me? You?"

"That would be me," I snap from his right.

He turns to face me, and I see his eyes widen as he takes us all in. "The fuck are you?"

"Should have done your research," I hiss. "Had you done, you'd have known that Mallory was never the target you should have gone for. She's not someone who's alone and vulnerable." I step forward. "You should never have touched her." I reach behind me, my fingers closing around the hilt of my blade.

It's easy and takes mere seconds. One minute he's watching me, the next, I'm jerking forward. Blade in hand, I thrust the knife into his stomach, close to where he stabbed Mallory months prior. The fucker hisses out a breath, his eyes wide and his jaw slack.

"Take him," I hiss. Right now, I need this cunt to be gone and away from here before Mallory comes out of her appointment.

"We've got this," Wrath assures me as Cowboy and Bozo reach for Micah and drag him toward the van that's parked in the parking lot. "I'll call Maverick. He'll want to be here when we deal with this bastard."

"Thanks, man."

He nods. "Your family's safe now, brother. Once you have them home, you can deal with this asshole."

I grit my teeth. I want to kill the fucker, but I have Mallory and Shay to care for right now. They are my main priority. Once I get them to the clubhouse, I'll let her know that she's safe. That we have Micah. She's not stupid; she knows exactly what I'm going to do to the bastard. Once the fucker's dead, she'll be able to sleep easy.

I hope.

I CLIMB off my bike and walk toward the fire. I have no doubt that it was Pyro who made this huge fucking bonfire. The fucker earned his moniker.

I need this shit done quickly. Once I got back to the clubhouse after Shay's appointment, I told Mallory about us finding Micah. The moment I told her we had him, she broke down. Her tears fucking tear me to pieces and I hate when she cries. She's shed so many fucking tears already.

"Yo, Rap," Py calls out, sitting on a fucking chair drinking a beer. "We've been waitin' on you."

"Had shit to deal with," I reply. "We ready?"

He gets to his feet. "Oh yeah, brother, we're ready. Maverick's here to ensure the body won't be found. The asshole is all yours, brother. Do what you've got to do. We're here to watch."

I chuckle as he retakes his seat, taking a sip of his beer. I glance to my left and see they've stripped Micah down to his pants. His hands are tied together and he's lying on his side. His body is already bruised. My brothers weren't holding back. This fucker's in a world of hurt already.

I pull off my cut and lay it on the empty chair my brothers have waiting for me. Everyone's here, including Maverick and Freddie. Stephen is at the hospital with Jess. She's recovering well from her burns and they reckon she'll be released in a few weeks.

I have spent countless hours contemplating what I will do to this despicable man. Multiple scenarios have played out in my mind—killing him swiftly, making him suffer with Stephen's infamous wood chipper method—but in the end, I know he deserves to pay for what he did to Mallory.

Without hesitation, I stalk toward him with a fierce determination. I've been dying for this day to arrive. I waste no time. My hand shoots out and clamps onto his arm, twisting it sharply and causing an audible pop as the joint dislocates from its socket. Satisfaction courses through me as I watch pain flash across his face, but it only fuels my desire for revenge. This is what he did to my woman. This is the pain he caused her.

With a firm grip on his now-useless arm, I haul him to his feet. He sways unsteadily at first but quickly regains his footing, his eyes never leaving mine as he glares back at me with grit and defiance. "What are you going to do?" he taunts, trying to mask the fear in his voice.

I draw back my arm and unleash my fury with a powerful punch that connects solidly with his jaw, sending him reeling backwards. The sound of bone against bone echoes through the air.

He continues to taunt me, but it's no use. His words mean fuck all to me. I unleash my rage upon him, grabbing him by the hair and yanking his head back. Exposing his vulnerable throat, I deliver another vicious punch, this time targeting his sternum. The force of the blow sends him crashing to the ground, the wind knocked out of him.

I stand over him, towering above him. I gaze down at the man who has been terrorizing the woman I love. The pain he caused my woman still burns within me like a raging fire. I won't stop, not until I kill him.

As he struggles to get back on his feet, I'm in such a dark haze that I don't even hesitate to slam my fist into his face.

Blood splatters across my knuckles as I strike, each blow bringing me closer to the release of all the pain and anger that has been festering inside me for far too long. But still, he refuses to stay down, continuing to defy me with his eyes full of hatred. It's time for his resolve to crumble.

I lash out with a series of kicks and punches, each one harder than the last. I'm relentless, losing myself in the violence as I pummel him into submission. I can see the life draining from his eyes, his breath growing ragged and shallow.

It's only a matter of moments before the fight will be over.

Finally, he's lying motionless on the ground. A small part of me wonders if Mallory's nightmares will still come even with his death. But she's not alone. She won't face them by herself if they do come.

"He's dead," Maverick says, stepping forward. "Mallory and Shay won't have to worry about him any longer. Now it's time to ensure that he's never found."

I leave Maverick be. He's been doing this shit for years. He's known as the Cleaner, and he's just as methodical as the Eraser. Both men are fucking ruthless in getting rid of their enemies.

I put my cut back on and take my seat. Pyro hands me a bottle of beer and I take it, before I sink into my seat and get set to enjoy the show.

Maverick sets up his equipment, a menacing bone saw clutched in one hand. He towers over the lifeless body of Micah with an insane grin on his face. With precise movements, he begins to hack away at Micah's limbs, sawing them off one by one. It's a disturbing sight, but I can't look away as the sound of bones cracking fills the air.

Each severed limb is placed carelessly on the ground, like a fucking serial killer with his trophies on display. No one makes a sound as he continues. We're all watching with rapt fascination.

As Maverick finishes his grisly work, he places the bone saw back into its case with a satisfied smirk. Streams of blood flow freely from the stumps of Micah's limbs, pooling on the grass beneath him. The smell of iron and flesh lingers heavy in the air. It's crazy, but at the same time, I'm unable to tear my gaze from the scene in front of me.

"What now?" Wrath asks, intrigue coating his words.

"Now," Maverick says with a wolfish grin, his eyes glinting with malice, "I make sure that his body will never be found." His movements are calculated and purposeful as he makes his way toward the shed. When he returns, he's carrying two large barrels, their metal surfaces gleaming in the dim light.

"The fuck are they for?" Wrath questions, his voice tinged with both disgust and curiosity.

"Wait and see, you impatient fuck," Maverick snaps, his tone laced with irritation.

As he approaches the barrels, I can't help but

wonder what else the barrels have been used for. I've heard the gruesome tales of what the Cleaner does—using strong chemicals to dissolve bodies until there's no trace left behind. It's a lengthy and disturbing process, one I have no doubt Maverick has used many times before throughout the country.

I sip on my drink as I watch him put Micah's limbs into the barrels. It's fucking weird, but I have to admit that these Irish fuckers are hardcore.

Maverick disappears for a moment, presumably back into the shed. When he returns, he's whistling an eerie tune that I can't quite place, but it sounds hauntingly similar to The Doors' "The End". In his hands, he carries a massive gallon bottle, no doubt filled with his chemical concoction.

The sound of him pouring the fluid into the barrels is mixed with the hissing and spitting of the fire. It just adds to the craziness of the night. Once he's finished, he slams the lids shut with a satisfying click and a wicked grin spreads across his face. Micah's fate has been sealed, his disappearance hidden within these barrels. No one is going to find Micah. Not fucking ever.

I stare at Maverick and realize that his laid back attitude is just a facade. He's a ruthless killer. It's no wonder this guy has a reputation for being one of the most ruthless and feared figures in the criminal underworld.

I rise to my feet. "It's time to go home. I appreciate your help, Maverick."

He shakes his head as he closes the gap between us. "We all dropped the ball on Mallory. We fucked up and she was left to deal with the pain from our failings. You know that whatever you need, I'm here."

I hold out my hand and he shakes it. "The same goes for you," I tell him, meaning the words I say. I may not be the most forthcoming but Maverick is a great ally, and I'll have his back no matter what.

He grins. "Go home, Rap, let Mallory know the cunt is gone. Maybe now she'll be able to mourn Jayne. Now she can live."

He's right. Maybe the knowledge that Micah's dead will help her out of the depths of her pain.

It's going to take time, but she's not alone. I'm going to be with her every fucking step of the way.

CHAPTER 25
MALLORY

TWELVE WEEKS LATER

"Hey, darlin', you okay?" Shane asks as he slides his arms around my waist. He presses his lips to my neck and I sink back against his embrace.

"Mmm," I moan, closing my eyes. "So good."

"Babe," he laughs. "I've had you twice this mornin'. I'm not as young as you and need time to recuperate."

I press my ass back against his groin, feeling his cock thicken beneath his jeans. "Seems to me like you don't need rest, old man."

Our relationship is beyond anything I could have ever dreamed. He's been at my side throughout my toughest days, and he's right beside me on the happiest ones too. I couldn't imagine this life without him. He came home the night he located Micah smelling of a bonfire. I didn't ask for details, afraid of the haunting images that would inevitably fill my mind. I couldn't let them in. I'd only start to feel sorrow for him.

Instead, he held me in his strong arms and made a promise to protect me from any further harm. And as his words washed over me, the walls I had built around my heart crumbled. The tears flowed freely then, for the loss of my mother, for all the time I had spent in hiding, and for the pain that had consumed me.

I have some bad days. When the pain of losing Ma hits me, it's hard to get out of bed, but I have Shay, who needs me, and I'm able to push the grief aside. My son will always know his granny. He'll always be told about the love she had for him.

"Babe," he growls, "I've got to get to work," he says thickly. "You're supposed to be at the clubhouse meeting Chloe."

"I know," I say as I turn to face him, wrapping my arms around his neck. "I love you," I tell him. I love him so deeply that I didn't think it was possible to feel so much for another person who isn't my child. But with Shane, the love I have is all-consuming. It's everything I could ever want. It's perfect.

He slides his hands into my hair, his forehead resting against mine. "The doctor will be by to check on you. I should be finished by the time she's at the clubhouse."

I grin, knowing I'm hiding something from him, something that Gráinne will be confirming today. I can't wait to tell him.

"Okay, go," I tell him, pressing a quick kiss to his lips. "I'll drive Shay and I to the clubhouse once I've fed him."

There's a moment of hesitation before he nods, still finding it difficult to let me go off alone. "Call me when you get there." His concern for my safety is clear in his voice, and I am more than willing to make this concession for him. I know how hard he searched for Micah, and the pain and anguish he felt when he couldn't find him. Sending him a text when I leave and calling him when I arrive is a small gesture that brings him some peace of mind.

"You've got it," I reassure him, placing another kiss on his lips. "Go on, honey. You need to go to work."

For just a few fleeting moments, when he disappears from sight, I am gripped by the bone-chilling fear that haunted me during my days in hiding. But then, like a soothing balm, the sound of his motorcycle engine revving fills the air and helps to erase that fear from my mind.

With a smile on my face, I turn and get back to making Shay's food, knowing that no matter what may come, Shane will always be there to chase away my fears and make me feel safe again.

"So, you were right," Gráinne says to me with a soft smile. "Is this good news or not?" she asks. "Are we celebrating or do we need to talk options?"

I shake my head, loving that she cares. Over the past three months, she's been at the clubhouse a lot more. She's now the club's official doctor, even though she's still in medical school. The brothers like her, as do the women, so it was a no-brainer on Pyro's part to have her be the club doctor.

"I'm happy. We'll definitely be celebrating," I tell her. "Now, are we going to talk about your face?" I ask. She's done a piss poor job of hiding the bruise that mars her jaw. Not to mention, there's a lot of swelling on her nose. "You've got a nasty bruise on your jaw, not to mention you've broken your nose."

She sighs, rubbing her hands together. "A patient got violent while I was working in the emergency room last week. Connor is going to lose his mind when he finds out."

"Hence the make-up?" I ask and she nods. "What's up with you two?"

"We've been friends since we were kids. Sometimes I feel like there's more and other times I want to kill him."

I laugh. "But?"

She shrugs. "But Connor is Connor and he's always kept me at arm's length."

My brows furrow. "Wait, have you two

ever..." I pause, trying to find the right words. "You know, been together?"

"We've had sex, sure, but it's easy for him to walk away." I see the tears in her eyes and my heart aches for her. "He's here and I see the club girls and it's driving me insane. I'm tired of being pushed aside, but I know if I say anything it'll just make him upset."

"I get it. Maybe it's time to move on?" I say. "You can't live in limbo all your life, Grá. It's not fair."

"You're right," she says with a grin. "You're dead right, Mal. There's a guy who's been asking me for a date and I keep saying no. But why should I put my life on hold when Connor has never given me a single indication that he wants anything more than friendship?"

Oh, I know Connor wants more. I've seen the way he looks at her. But a man like him isn't going to do anything until he finds out he's about to lose her.

"Then go on that date. Go have some fun. You deserve it, Grá."

The sound of pipes reaches us and I can't help but smile. Shane's home.

She rises to her feet. "I should go," she tells me.

"No, stay, please," I urge. "I want you to be here when I tell Shane."

She beams at me. "Are you sure?"

I nod. "Definitely. In fact, you can tell him. He's going to ask you if everything's okay and I'm giving you full support in telling him."

She reaches for my hand and laughs. "He's going to be delighted with himself. He's such a good dad to Shay."

The doors open and in walks Shane, Pyro, and Bozo. "Darlin'," Shane greets me. "Everythin' okay?"

I nod. "Yeah, I'm good. Just catching up with Grá."

Shane's gaze swings to Gráinne. "Doc, everythin' okay with her?"

I give her a small nod and she clasps her hands together. "Yes, Raptor, her pregnancy is coming along perfectly."

I swear, you could hear a pin drop with how quiet the room has fallen.

"Wanna repeat that?" Shane growls before he turns to me. "You're pregnant?"

"Surprise," I say weakly. "Yeah, honey, we're having another baby."

He closes the distance between us and hauls me into his arms. His lips descend on mine. The kiss is hot and heavy, and I cling to him, unable to trust my feet as he's made my knees weak and my toes curl with the kiss.

"And that's my cue to leave," Grá says, laughing. "Mallory, I'll speak to you later."

"The fuck happened to your face?" I hear Bozo growl.

I pull back from Shane and see Bozo holding on to Grá's arm, his gaze intense as he takes in her bruised face. "I'm fine," she insists, wrenching her arm from his grip.

"Fine my ass. Fuck, Grá, what the hell?"

She shakes her head. "I've got to go."

"Grá, call me and let me know how the date goes," I say loudly.

Her eyes widen and she ducks her head and hurries from the room. Bozo glares at me. "What date?" he snarls.

I cross my arms over my chest and glare right back at him. Shane's arms slide around my waist and he holds me against his chest. "She's not going to wait around for you to get your head out of your ass, Bozo. You don't want her, fine, but someone else does. Leave her alone and let her be happy."

Just like any other biker, he shakes his head and prowls after his woman. I have no doubt that Grá will be going on a date, but it won't be with the guy who's been asking her out. Not now. Bozo's just been given the nudge he needed.

Pyro's cell rings, breaking through the silence of us watching the door while waiting for Bozo to return. "What's up?" he answers. His face changes from mildly annoyed to furious. "I'll be there soon."

"What's happened?" Shane asks.

"That was Denis," Pyro hisses. "Maverick's been taken. I'm going to meet up with him and find out what's happened. Once I know, we'll start to search for him."

My heart sinks. What? Oh fuck, who's taken him?

"We're goin' to bed to celebrate," Shane says, his breath hot against my neck, pulling me from my thoughts of Maverick. "There's nothing we can do right now and we're not going to have much time to celebrate, but I need you."

I inwardly squeal. God yes. The way Shane and I celebrate, it's going to be amazing.

He takes my hand and begins to lead me upstairs.

I'm so fucking happy, and I know Ma is happy for me too. This is all she wanted for me. I wish she could have witnessed this, but I know she's looking down from heaven and smiling.

GLOSSARY

Here's a glossary of how to pronounce some of the names/words in this book:

Gráinne's: pronounced: graw-nyuh
Ailbhe: pronounced: Al-vuh
Mo ghrá: pronounced: moh graw

Are you ready for more?

UP NEXT IS BOZO'S STORY.

Here's the tropes you'll find in Bozo and Gráinne's story

Friends to lovers
Unexpected pregnancy
Heroine in Danger
Touch her and die vibes
MC romance

BOOKS BY BROOKE:

The Kingpin Series:

Forbidden Lust

Dangerous Secrets

Forever Love

The Made Series:

Bloody Union

Unexpected Union

Fragile Union

Shattered Union

Hateful Union

Vengeful Union

Explosive Union

Cherished Union

Obsessive Union

Gallo Famiglia:

Ruthless Arrangement

Ruthless Betrayal

Ruthless Passion

The Houlihan Men of Dublin:

The Eraser

The Cleaner

The Silencer

The Fury Vipers MC NY Chapter:

Stag

Mayhem

Digger

Ace

Pyro

Shadow

Wrath

Reaper

The Fury Vipers MC Dublin Chapter:

Preacher

Raptor

Bozo

Standalones:

Saving Reli

Taken By Nikolai

A Love So Wrong

His Dark Desire*

OTHER PEN NAMES

Stella Bella

(A forbidden Steamy Pen name)

Taboo Temptations:

Wicked With the Professor

Snowed in with Daddy

Wooed by Daddy

Loving Daddy's Best Friend

Brother's Glory

Daddy's Curvy Girl

Daddy's Intern

His Curvy Brat

His Curvy Temptress

Daddy's Devilish Girl

Twisted Daddy

Seduced by Daddy's Best Friend

Stepbrother Seduction

Taboo Teachings:

Royally Taught

Extra Curricular with Mr. Abbot

Forbidden Bosses:

Conveniently Yours

Bred by Daddy

Gilded Billionaire

Maid for Love

One Night Forever

His Dark Desire*

* Crossover novella with the Made Series by Brooke Summers and the Forbidden Bosses Series by Stella Bella

ABOUT BROOKE SUMMERS:

USA Today Bestselling Author Brooke Summers is a Mafia Romance author and is best known for her Made Series.

Brooke lives with her daughter and hubby on the picturesque west coast of Ireland. There's nothing Brooke loves more than spending time with her family and exploring new cities.

Want to know more about Brooke? www.brookesummersbooks.com
Subscribe to her newsletter: www.brookesummersbooks.com/newsletter
Join Brooke's Babes Facebook group.

Printed in Great Britain
by Amazon